MAX-PLANCK-GESELLSCHAFT

Universität
Augsburg
University

TECHNISCHE
UNIVERSITÄT
MÜNCHEN

THE GEORGE
WASHINGTON
UNIVERSITY

WASHINGTON, DC

MIPLC Studies
Edited by

Prof. Dr. Christoph Ann, LL.M. (Duke Univ.)
Technische Universität München

Prof. Robert Brauneis
The George Washington University Law School

Prof. Dr. Josef Drexl, LL.M. (Berkeley)
Max Planck Institute for Innovation and Competition

Prof. Dr. Michael Kort
University of Augsburg

Prof. Dr. Thomas M.J. Möllers
University of Augsburg

Prof. Dr. Dres. h.c. Joseph Straus
Max Planck Institute for Innovation and Competition

Volume 24

Carl Dominik J. Niedersüß

I Don't Even Recognize You Anymore

The Limits of the Protection of Alteration and
Modernisation of Fictitious Characters

MIPLC Munich Augsburg
Intellectual München
Property Washington DC
Law Center

Die Deutsche Nationalbibliothek lists this publication in the
Deutsche Nationalbibliografie; detailed bibliographic data
is available in the Internet at http://dnb.d-nb.de

a.t.: Munich, Munich Intellectual Property Law Center, Thesis "Master of Laws in Intellectual Property (LL.M. IP)", 2013

ISBN   978-3-8487-1545-9 (Print)
        978-3-8452-5714-3 (ePDF)

British Library Cataloguing-in-Publication Data
A catalogue record for this book is available from the British Library.

ISBN   978-3-8487-1545-9 (Print)
        978-3-8452-5714-3 (ePDF)

Library of Congress Cataloging-in-Publication Data
Niedersüß, Carl Dominik J.
I Don't Even Recognize You Anymore
The Limits of the Protection of Alteration and Modernisation of Fictitious Characters
Carl Dominik J. Niedersüß
72 p.
Includes bibliographic references.

ISBN   978-3-8487-1545-9 (Print)
        978-3-8452-5714-3 (ePDF)

1. Edition 2015
© Nomos Verlagsgesellschaft, Baden-Baden, Germany 2015. Printed and bound in Germany.

Dedicated to the loving memory of Emil Dominik Neidenbach.

D A# B G A A#-B-A#-B-A#-B D'
A# B G A#-B-D'-E'-D'-B A
A# B G A A#-B-A#-B-A#-B D'
E'-E'-E'-E'-D'-B G A H G A G

Abstract

This paper addresses the legal issues that arise in the registration and use of advertising characters. The notion of "advertising characters" in this context is to be distinguished from the traditional "mascot", as it includes human or anthropomorphic fictional characters that appear in advertising and marketing materials for a given product or service, or are being used for merchandising purposes. They are not limited to a mere graphical depiction, but moreover exhibit additional features such as character traits, voices and behaviour.

In recent years, the advertisement industry has been increasingly relying on the use of this type of characters for creating brand images. Reasons for this development are not only to be found in the availability of more sophisticated graphical representations following great advancements in the creation of CGI (and their popularity in the general audience), but also in the stronger incorporation of psychological theory in advertisement. In addition to that, they have come to generate considerable merchandising revenues.

While seldom operated independently of traditional trade marks, advertisement characters have become an important complement to them, adding substantial value to the overall brand image. Advertising characters have enormous recognition and identification value, and bear higher integrability in interactive marketing measures, and more importantly in modern social media, than conventional marks. Needless to say, their creation is connected with substantial investments.

This paper aspires to thoroughly analyse the eligibility for protection under traditional trade mark law, paying special attention to their intangible properties such as character traits, voices and behaviour. Furthermore, it will address the scope of their protection. Departing from trade mark law, this paper will also cover adjacent matters especially copyright law and unfair competition. While focussing on the legal situations in the U.S. and in Germany, it also mentions noteworthy European decisions and the Community Trade Mark regime.

Table of Contents

Acronyms and Abbreviations

AIPPI	International Association for the Protection of Industrial Property
BIRP	United International Bureaux for Protection of Intellectual Property
CGI	Computer Generated Imagery
CJEU	Court of Justice of the European Union
CTM	Community Trade Mark
CTMR	Community Trade Mark Regulation
GC	General Court of the European Union
GCA	German Copyright Act
IPR	Intellectual Property Rights
OHIM	Office for the Harmonization of the Internal Market
UCA	German Unfair Competition Act
USPTO	United States Patent and Trademark Office
WIPO	World Intellectual Property Organisation

I. Introduction

"Unlike most paintings, photographs or novelty items, a character can take on a life of its own, and thus may be protected against copies in postures, settings and attitudes far removed from any in the author's original depiction".[1]

In a multitude of ways, fictitious characters are being employed in the marketing of goods: Be it as spokes-characters in advertisement campaigns, or be it by adding substantial value to bulk products in ways of merchandising. Characters are semantic units consisting of name, visual appearance, voice and an underlying scheme of personality traits and experiences. And just by their mere presence, they are able to serve as designators of source. It is because of their complex structure and their relative novelty, that characters are rarely granted clear-cut protection as such under one IP right, but benefit from a historically grown patchwork of protection for selected aspects.

In recent years, the advertisement industry has been increasingly reliant on the use of these advertising characters in the creation of brand images. Reasons for this development are not only to be found more sophisticated graphical representations following great advancements in the creation of CGI (and their popularity in the general audience), but also in the stronger incorporation of psychological theory in advertisement. Characters are able to create more trust than traditional brands, thus selling more products. Advertising characters have enormous recognition and identification value, and bear higher integrability in interactive marketing measures, and more importantly in modern social media, than conventional marks. Needless to say, their creation is connected with substantial investments.

But just like their human models, fictitious characters are not static but are subject to constant evolutionary change, be it in reply to a market demand, or as a logical consequence of reasons inherent to the character's structure. This leads to difficulties in distinction not only

---

1 Paul Goldstein & P. Berndt Hugenholtz, International Copyright: Principles, Law and Practice § 2.11.3. at 158 (2d ed. 2010).

whether protection is to be awarded at all, or in the determination when a threshold of protection is met, but also to what degree the protection of these alterations can be tucked to the object originally protected.

My goal is to thoroughly analyse the eligibility for protection under traditional trade mark law and adjacent matters, paying special attention to the protection of character changes, modernisation and alteration.

II. General considerations

A. Character advertisement

1. Definition of the notion "character"

A character is a fictitious person, able to independently communicate and interact with its surroundings. Fictional characters consist of manifold components that may be classified in different ways.[2] Most common is the attribution of a name, a physical or visual appearance and personality traits or character features,[3] but the presence of all of these features is not imperatively necessary to constitute a character in this sense.

It shall be clarified, that this definition also encompasses characters portrayed by actual actors, visualized by two or three dimensional graphics, literally described, and even lacking visual appearance all-together. Hence "spokes-characters" and "mascots" are covered, and even speech based personal assistance software for cellphones may qualify as character in this sense, as long as it has a distinct personality trait such as witty sense of humour. Furthermore, while this often will be the case, characters must not necessarily be human or anthropo-morphic. This definition will cover characters created merely for the purpose of advertisement, and characters originally created for other purposes – most noteworthy entertainment – that are later being used

---

2 E. Fulton Brylawski, *Protection of Characters – Sam Spade revisited*, 22 Bull. Copyright Soc'y 77, 78 (1974); see also *infra* note 8 at 127.

3 *Id.*; Michael V. P. Marks, *The Legal rights of Fictional Characters,* 25 Copyright L. Symp. (ASCAP) 35, 37-38 (1980); *see also* Thiele *infra* note 25 at 431; David B. Feldman, *Finding a Home for Fictional Characters: A Proposal for Change in Copyright Protection*, 78 Calif. L. Rev. 687, 690.

for advertisement purposes.[4] In cases where the border between fiction and reality is fuzzy,[5] characters will be assumed to be fictitious.

My intent is to approach the topic from a trade mark point of view, thus focusing the analysis on characters that are being used in combination with the marketing of goods and services, independent of the question whether the use may serve the purpose of an indicator of origin. I will refer to all of these practises as "character marketing".

While this definition covers both characters that were created for the purpose of advertisement and characters that were originally created for entertainment purposes, economic considerations may call for a fundamentally different treatment of those two categories. The term "character merchandising", may, depending on the definition, refer to a variety of business practises on a spectrum between "the economic exploitation of a character",[6] "use of distinctive elements to enhance the promotion or sale of products",[7] and the mere decoration of bulk articles with images of popular characters.[8] According to the definition, the character may or may not serve a designator of commercial origin. Character merchandising is only one of the motivations for character protection, but not the sole one. However, as I will show below, character protection solely for the sake of merchandising may be inconsistent with some intellectual property right's economical foundations.

---

4 WIPO, *Character Merchandising – Report Prepared by the International Bureau*, WO/INF/108 (Dec.1994).
5 The Marx Brothers, and once-fictitious-turned-real rock icons Spinal Tap come to mind as examples.
6 Matthias Meyer, *Character Merchandising, Der Schutz fiktiver Figuren als Marke* [*Character Merchandising, The Protection of Fictitious Characters as Trade Marks*], Europäische Hochschulschriften: Reihe 2, Rechtswissenschaft, volume 3668 (Ger.).
7 See *infra* note 18 at 2.
8 Christian Scherz & Susanne Bergmann, *Character Merchandising in Germany in* Character Merchandising in Europe (Heijo Ruijsenaars ed., 2003), 127-143, 128.

2. Reasons for character marketing

For more than a century, advertisers have been relying on spokes-characters as a means of communication that is able to generate a large degree of customer attention and sympathy while in the meantime transporting marketing messages.[9]

Spokes-characters essentially serve the same purposes as trade marks, namely indication of origin, guarantee of quality and marketing and advertising, the latter with significant advantages towards traditional marks: Studies have shown, that spokes-characters, more so than other vehicles of communication, have an impact customer's willingness to buy, by positively influencing customer's attitude towards a product or brand.[10] Trust in the character as well as sympathy for and attractiveness of the character directly effect the appeal of a product.[11] Spokes-characters can be perceived as experts, able to make valid claims or having knowledge on a product's quality, generating trust.[12] Surveys suggest, that children display higher attentiveness when watching commercials in which spokes-characters are involved.[13] In addition to that, spokes-characters may stimulate nostalgia in consumers who had been exposed to them in an early age. Not unlike TV-shows that are set in the past in the attempt to emotionally bring people back to a "simpler time", marketing characters can profit from this appeal.[14] Long-term use of spokes-characters may

---

9 Frank Lotze, *Markenmaskottchen – Warum wir bestimmte Werbefiguren nie vergessen* [*Spokescharacters – Why Certain Marketing Characters are Never Forgotten*], Welt am Sonntag, Jul 22nd 2012.

10 Frank Huber, Kai Vollhardt & Frederick Meyer, *Helden der Werbung? – Eine Untersuchung der Relevanz von Werbefiguren für das Konsumverhalten* [*Heroes of Advertisement? – Research on the Relevance of Spokes-Characters for Consumers' Behaviour*], Marketing volume 31, no. 03, (2009) (Ger.).

11 *Id.*

12 Judith Garretson & Roland Niedrich, *Spokes-Characters – Creating Character Trust and Positive Brand Attitudes*, Journal of Advertising, volume 33, no. 2 (2004), 25-36 at 27.

13 *Id.*

14 *Id.* at 27 et seq.

trigger customer nostalgia, raising customer's impression of character's trustworthiness.[15]

More so than regular brands, they enjoy widespread recognition, and are able to penetrate everyday life by being the subject of conversation, or as one may even say: "The Budweiser frogs and the Taco Bell Chihuahua ... are public figures every bit as ubiquitous in some circles as Oprah Winfrey, Leonardo DiCaprio or William Jefferson Clinton".[16] As opposed to celebrity testimonials, artificial spokescharacters are comparably cheap in maintenance and do not bear the risk of causing negative publicity due to despicable behaviour outside the advertisement context.

In addition to that, they are social-media friendly, facilitating direct communication with individuals on a large scale. Individuals will not have to befriend anonymous undertakings, but more accessible characters.

Particularly as to character merchandising, in the meaning of "the secondary exploitation, by the creator of a character or by a real person or by one of several authorized third parties, of the essential personality features of a character in relation to various goods and/or services, with a view to creating in prospective consumers a desire to acquire those goods and/or to use those services because of the consumers' affinity to that character",[17] another motivation for character advertising becomes evident: If a character has established a reputation in its first domain of use, its owner may capitalize on this reputation in secondary domains of use.[18] Depending on the fame of the characters involved, substantial revenues may be generated with character merchandising. Disney, generating almost as much income in

---

15 *Id.*
16 See *infra* note 131 at 1732.
17 Heijo Ruijsenaars, *The WIPO Report on Character Merchandising*, Int'l. Rev. of Intell. Prop. and Competition Law [IIC] 1994, 532, 532 (1994); *see also supra* note 4.
18 Heijo Ruijsenaars, *Overview of the Legal Aspects of Merchandising in* Character Merchandising in Europe (Heijo Ruijsenaars ed., 2003), 2.

merchandising as in global movie distribution in 2010, serves as a prime example.[19]

While apparently fictional characters have grown substantially in value over the past decades, their owners have responded with creative legal solutions to provide protection for this value and the investment necessary in order to build it up.[20] Or, as *Helfland* argues, "aggressive protection is spurred on by the near human quality inherent in these beings."[21]

3. The need to adapt

While it would be far from the truth to say that conventional trade marks do not change at all, characters are essentially different in two ways: Firstly, a character that is in use, be it in a work of art or as a mere marketing vehicle, is always also evolving in a certain way. Every bit of interaction with its surroundings or with other characters, defines the acting character more precisely, thus ultimately changing it from more vague to more sophisticated. Characters that have been around for a while, reach levels of sophistication far beyond all other categories of trade marks, including those of highly abstract types of nonconventional marks.

In addition to this development, characters have been a major means of market communication since their rise in last century's seventies. Many well-known advertisement characters have clocked in significant amounts of service time. "Mickey Mouse", "Superman", "Tony the Tiger" and "Bibendum"[22] for example all have been used in commerce for more than 60 years. In view of this tendency towards longevity, adaptation and modernization is an inherent necessity for a multitude of reasons. Firstly, a modern and appealing appearance

---

19 $ 28,6 billion, see License! Global Magazine, May 18th 2011.

20 Michael T. Helfland, *When Mickey Mouse is as strong as Superman: The Convergence of Intellectual Property Laws to Protect Fictional Literary and Pictorial Characters*, 44 Stan. L. Rev. 623, 624.

21 *Id.*

22 *A.k.a.* "The Michelin Man".

calls for regular visual streamlining resulting in graphical overhauls. Secondly, on a related note, changes in consumer demand or in the general zeitgeist may require characters to change, in order to maintain their appeal. Mickey Mouse again may serve as a prime example: In his first appearance on the silver screen, "Steamboat Willie",[23] Disney's rodent behemoth was portrayed in a physical appearance almost identical to the one it has today. Its character traits, voice, and behaviour, however, have changed significantly. And justly so, because nowadays a character force feeding a cow or deliberately torturing multiple animals by abusing them as musical instruments probably would not represent the image and values a family entertainment company is aiming for. Thirdly, new corporate strategies such as new product groups sold by the sign holder may necessitate brand repositioning, resulting in the editing of character features.

The AIPPI recognised this need for adaptation of marketing characters and included a corresponding policy recommendation in the 1993 resolution, calling for the "copyright laws (to) be applied or interpreted, and if necessary modified, to permit protection against minor variations or modifications of the elements used in merchandising."[24]

B. Legal considerations on character advertisement

Characters, unlike most other signs used in commerce do not consist of one single, homogenous element, but at best are the coherent composition of a multitude of elements, including the visual appearance and dress style, name, personality traits, background story and upbringing, voice and accent, movement, and behavioural patterns. All of these elements are theoretically capable of being per se distinctive of a character, thus enabling coattail riders to create mental associations with an entire character, by imitating just one of these elements. Furthermore, all of these features can be subject to change due

---

23 *Cf.: Steamboat Willie*, Disney Brothers Studio (1928).
24 Heijo Ruijsenaars, *Workshop No. 6 – Character Merchandising*, AIPPI Y.B. 1992/III, 348. *See also supra* note 18 at 9.

to modernisation or character development. Moreover, characters are not bound to one single depiction or medium, but can be made accessible by word, writing or graphical depiction, and are accessible to interpretation by actors.[25]

As I will show below, some regimes award protection to characters per se, meaning to the entirety of features that constitute a character. Other regimes however, most notably the trade mark system, do not recognize the protection of characters as such, necessitating an analysis with regard to every single feature forming the character.

Furthermore, with such a multitude of aspects in question, and cumulative protection under several regimes being in general possible,[26] significant overlaps of protection through different regimes of Intellectual Property law may occur. In 1992, the AIPPI issued a resolution on the legal aspects of character merchandising,[27] also recommending trade mark protection as primary means to establish character rights. The rationale behind this recommendation is a pragmatic one, since it is often impossible to distinguish between characters that are being used as trade marks, and characters that only augment the eye-appeal of goods.[28] At the same time, the AIPPI clarified that character merchandising is not exclusively a trade mark matter.[29] Reasons to resort to different regimes of protection include compensation for the lack of a certain type of protection (e.g. copyright protection has expired, so the rights holder resorts to trade mark protection), or a wider scope of protection of a certain regime (e.g. opposed act is covered by copyright fair use, but trade mark provides a remedy against it).

---

25 See also: Clemens Thiele, *Urheberrechtlicher Schutz für Kunstfiguren – von Odysseus bis Lara Croft [Copyright Protection for Fictitious Characters – From Odysseus to Lara Croft]*, Legal Observations of the European Audiovisual Observatory [IRIS], 431, 437 (2004).

26 See also: Boston Professional Hockey Association, Inc. v. Dallas Cap & Emblem Mfg., Inc. 510 F.2d 1004, 1010 et seq. (5th. Cir. 1975).

27 *See supra* note 24.

28 *See* supra note 18 at 4.

29 *Id.* at 6.

As to the legal permissability of character adaptations, the International legal framework, notably Article 5 Section C paragraph 2 of the Paris Convention[30] provides some guidance for the relevant jurisdictions:

"Use of a trade mark by the proprietor in a form differing in elements which do not alter the distinctive character of the mark in the form in which it was registered in one of the countries of the Union shall not entail invalidation of the registration and shall not diminish the protection granted to the mark."

The convention thus allows for unessential differences, e.g. the adaptation or translation of marks, and differences in form, so long as these changes do not alter the distinctive character of the mark. The question, whether the distinctive character of a mark is preserved, is to be assessed by the competent national authorities, and will be analysed below.[31] The convention not only forbids invalidation of the mark, but also diminishment of the protection granted to it, meaning signs altered in accordance with the above criteria must be considered as having been used in their original form.[32] Whether the altered form enters into consideration in terms of infringement, depends on the national jurisdiction of the country concerned.[33]

In order to be able to treat the different regimes in depth, I shall limit the scope of this paper to the regimes of trade mark, copyright, unfair competition and personality protection or the right to publicity respectively.

C. *Economic considerations on character advertisement*

The U.S. and the continental European approach to justifying copyright protection vary significantly. While the latter historically emphasises the importance of moral justifications for Copyright protec-

---

30 Paris Convention for the Protection of Industrial Property Art. 5, Mar. 20, 1883, 21 U.S.T. 1583, 828 U.N.T.S. 305.
31 Georg Bodenhausen, Guide to the Application of the Paris Convention for the Protection of Industrial Property, Art. 5 (C) 2 (g) (BIRPI 1969).
32 *Id.* at Art. 5 (C) 2 (i).
33 *Id. See also infra* note 83.

tion, be those based on Locke's theory that labour creates entitlement to its fruits or on Hegel's considerations, interpreting property as the natural right to man. U.S. scholars traditionally have remained sceptical towards these justifications,[34] emphasising the economic justifications underlying copyright protection. The United States economic system is most commonly described by the fundamental notion that public welfare is best advanced by free competition.[35] Allowing competitors to freely copy products and services leads to lower costs, better features and reduces prices.[36]

Both systems share the belief, that artists as well as investors are responsible for the dissemination of the works may be reluctant to invest in creative activities without a regime of decent protection, allowing them to recoup the investment in creation.[37] Authors might forego development of their ideas, or distribute works through secret channels – both preventing public benefit from the creation that they otherwise might have enjoyed.[38]

The copyright system intends to solve this problem by granting artists a limited period of exclusivity, giving them an opportunity to profit from their creativity before facing free competition.[39] Theoretically, the duration of protection granted is to be appropriately regulated as to grant sufficient reward, but not overprotect the work.[40] After expiration of the protection, the work enters into the public domain. This mechanism has become known as the copyright trade-off.

While there is a wide consensus that trade marks are intended to serve an alltogether different role,[41] their nature in detail has been the

---

34 William Landes & Rrichard Posner, The Economic Structure of Intellectual Property Law, 5 et seq. (Harvard University Press 2003).
35 *See:* E. Wine Corp. v. Winslow-Warren, Ltd. 137 F.2d 955, 958 (2d Cir. 1943); Bonito Boats, Inc. v. Thunder Craft Boats, Inc. 489 U.S. 141, 146 (1989).
36 Lee Burgunder, *Trademark Registration of Product Colours: Issues and Answers*, 26 Santa Clara L.Rev. 581, 583 (1986).
37 *See generally*: Paul Goldstein, *The Competitive Mandate: From Sears to Lear*, 59 Cal. L. Rev. 873, 878 (1971).
38 *See infra* note 215 at 267.
39 *Id.*
40 *See generally supra* note 34 at chapter 3 – A Formal Model for copyright.
41 TrafFix Devices, Inc. v. Mktg. Displays Inc., 532 U.S. 23, 34 (2001).

the subject of debate.[42] Even though the CJEU has acknowledged other, more opaque functions of trade marks, including those of quality, communication, advertisement and investement,[43] their essential function is still considered to be "to guarantee the identity of the origin of the trade-marked product."[44] Thus, trade marks intend to give companies exclusive rights to identification symbols, in order to allow consumers to distinguish their products as to their commercial source.[45] Hence the public benefit deriving from the protection of trade symbols is the prevention of consumer confusion,[46] improving efficiency without raising competitive roadblocks.[47] Be they considered as property rights or not,[48] the purpose of their protection is to grant a right over a clearly defined sign. Otherwise, the grant of protection, and the possibility to monopolize would unduly interfere with public interests. Consumers mentally connect a certain sign with a commercial origin. Assuming that in general alterations of trade marks also cause some sort of rupture to this mental connection, it is evident that a consistent sign is more apt to prevent likelihood of confusion. However, the strength of a sign, meaning its appeal to customers, will positively affect its capability to act a designator of origin. Thus, the protection of character adaptations will have to be judged in the context of the delicate interaction between those two factors, and the public interest of limiting rights conferred by trade marks to a minimum extent.

Besides their main function as indicator of source, trade marks have intrinsic worth that is different from the goodwill in the products they

---

42 *See generally* Ilanah Simon, *How does "Essential Function" Drive European Trade Mark Law? What is the Essential Function of a Trade Mark?* 2005 IIC 401.
43 Case C-487/07, L'Oréal SA et. al. v. Bellure NV et. al. 2009 E.C.R. I-5185, para 58.
44 Case C-102/77, Hoffmann-La Roche & Co., AG et. al v. Centrapharm Vertriebsgesellschaft Pharmazeutischer Erzeugnisse, m.b.H. 1978 E.C.R. 1139, para 7.
45 See infra note 215 at 269.
46 *See generally:* Ralph Brown, *Advertising and the Public Interest, Legal Protection of Trade Symbols*, 57 Yale L.J. 1206 (1948); Jessica Litman, *Breakfast with Batman: The Public Interest in the Advertising Age*, 108 Yale L.J. 1717.
47 *Id* at 1719.
48 *See e.g.* Prestonettes, Inc. v. COTY, 264 U.S. 359, 368-369 (1924).

differentiate:[49] "Warner Bros. have brought out a seemingly endless series of lackluster Batman sequels. Critics disliked the sequels and their box offices performances were mediocre, but the sales of Batman toys have more than made up for it."[50] Considering the vast revenues generated by merchandising, one could argue that these serve as an incentive to create in themselves, capable of acting as an alternative to, or even a factual replacement of copyright law.

Finally, it must be pointed out that, given the consent of the author, trade mark law in general allows for the use of signs protected by copyright law. The doctrine of dilution has extended the protection of marks beyond likelihood of confusion, and has promoted them to a property-like state. Thus under certain circumstances, trade mark protection is able to perpetuate the protection of original works of authorship for a single source, rendering the copyright trade-off ineffective, by granting a monopoly to a certain content, without providing any benefits for the general public. I will analyse recent jurisdiction dealing with this problem.

---

49 *See* Litman *supra* note 46 at 1729.
50 *Id.* at 1726. Although, admittedly, "The Dark Knight" (2008) was a turning point in terms of critical acclaim and box office success.

III. Germany and the European Union

A. Trade mark protection

1. Protection in the national German framework

Trade mark law has been substantially harmonised throughout the European Union with the implementation of the Trade Mark Directive of 1995.[51] While the German system does offer protection for non-registered trade marks, it does so only in peculiar circumstances, most noteworthy that more than 50% of the public must be aware of the sign.[52] The vast majority of cases therefore require federal registration. As to the duration, trade marks are "potentially perpetual dependent upon continued use and distinctiveness".[53]

Section 3 (1) of the German Trade Mark Act describes the signs eligible for trade mark protection: "All signs, particularly words including personal names, designs, letters, numerals, sound marks, three-dimensional designs, the shape of goods or their packaging, as well as other wrapping including colours and colour combinations, may be protected as trade marks if they are capable of distinguishing the goods and services of one enterprise from those of other enterprises."[54] While this list of trade mark varieties is not exhaustive,[55] it does explicitly provide for the most significant means of character protection, namely the protection of the graphic representations and

---

51 Directive 2008/95/EC, of the European Parliament and the Council af 22 October 2008 to approximate the Laws of the Member States Relating to Trade Marks, O.J. (L 299) 25 – "Trade Mark Directive".

52 Gesetz über den Schutz von Marken und sonstigen Kennzeichen [Markengesetz] [MarkenG][Trade Marks Act], Jan 1st 1995, Bundesgesetzblatt [BGBl] 1 S 2302, 2310 as amended § 4 para. 2.

53 Graeme Dinwoodie, *Trademark and Copyright: Complements or Competitors?*, Proceedings of the ALAI Congress, June 13-17, 2001, 517.

54 *Id.* § 3 para. 1, translation provided by the German Federal Ministry of Justice, translation by Brian Duffett and Neil Mussett; *Cf.* Directive 2008/95/EC, Art 2.

55 Karl-Heinz Fezer, Markenrecht § 3 at 2 (4th ed. 2009).

names of characters.[56] Even the names of famous literary characters in the public domain are eligible for trade mark protection, with the exception of genericism of names, meaning cases in which a character's most characteristic personality features have become generic expressions for a certain kind of character.[57]

The protection of phonetic aspects of a character is limited by the fact, that the German trade mark system does not allow for sound marks in the form of spoken word, but only as non-lingual sounds perceivable by human ears.[58] Voices that are accompanied by background music are considered non-lingual in that sense. Additionally, the characteristics of a voice are eligible for protection.[59]

In order to be eligible for protection, signs must meet three general requirements: The mark has to (1) be a sign in the legal sense,[60] (2) possess abstract distinctiveness,[61] and (3) be able to be represented graphically.[62] While the question what a sign in the legal sense is, is disputed,[63] the most common approach – influenced by modern marketing theory – interprets trade marks as dynamic systems of communication between customers and undertakings, allowing for most signs to be eligible for trade mark protection.[64] This seems to be in accordance with the CJEU's recent jurisdiction, enabling a wide array of mark types.[65]

A further requirement is the uniformity of the sign: Signs that can be represented by more than one manifestation are not eligible pro-

---

56 *Id.* § 15 at 259; *supra* note 8 at 131.
57 *See supra* note 55 § 8 at 292, e.g. Don Quichotte, Werther, Sherlock Holmes.
58 *See also supra* note 55 § 3 at 591.
59 See supra note 55 § 3 at 595.
60 Ger: "Zeichen im Rechtssinne".
61 Ger: "Abstrakte Unterscheidungseignung".
62 Ger: "Graphische Darstellbarkeit".
63 *See supra* note 55 § 3 at 324.
64 *Id.*
65 *Cf.* Case C-273/00, Ralf Sieckmann v. Deutsches Patent- und Markenamt, 2002 E.C.R. I-11737; Case C-299/99, Koninklijke Philips Electronics NV v. Remington Consumer Products Ltd, 2002 E.C.R. I-5475; Case C-104/01, Libertel Groep BV v. Benelux Merkenbureau, 2003 E.C.R. I-3793; Case C-283/01, Shield Mark BV v. Joost Kist, 2003 E.C.R. I-14313.

tection.[66] This slams the door shut on the protection of complex personality traits and accents, whose inherent nature is that they are not uniformly manifested, unless they are reduced to an overly simple, uniform and predetermined scheme. Aim of the graphical representation requirement is the unambiguous fixation of the mark's properties, to allow for publicity and identifiability of the sign.[67] The European Commission has recently published a proposal[68] to eliminate the latter requirement, and instead to demand the sign "being represented in a manner which enables the competent authorities and the public to determine the precise subject of the protection afforded to its proprietor." The realisation of this proposal would enshrine the uniformity requirement, as is already in force in Germany, in the rest of the Union, and limit personality trait's registrability to the above described minimum.

Section 14 of the Trade Marks Act directly transposes Art 5 of Directive 89/104 into German Law, by prohibiting third parties from using (1) identical signs for identical goods and services (so called "double identity"), (2) confusingly similar signs, and (3) diluting well-known signs in ways of blurring, tarnishment or free-riding. The CJEU has held that in cases of double identity, likelihood of confusion is not necesssary for a behaviour to constitute infringement, as long as one of the trade mark's functions "such as, in particular, [the] function of communication, investment or advertisement" is affected.[69] Furthermore, trade mark infringement requires the use of the sign as a trade mark. According to recent jurisdiction of the CJEU and the

---

66 *See supra* note 55 § 3 at 328; *cf. also* Case C-321/03 Dyson v. Registrar of Trademarks, 2007 E.C.R. I-687 at 37 (CJEU).

67 *See supra* note 55 § 3 at 389 et seq.

68 Proposal for a Directive of the European Parliament and of the Council to Approximate the Laws of the Member States Relating to Trade marks, COM (2013) 162 final, 2013/0089 (COD), (proposed 2013).

69 Case C-487/07, L'Oréal v. Bellure, para 63.

BGH however, the threshold for trade mark use is rather low,[70] including every use of a sign for the purpose of the sale of goods or services, in connection with the mark's original function as a designator of origin.

In addition to conventional (and non-conventional) trade mark protection, the Trade Mark Act grants sui generis protection to the titles of works.[71] This protection, originally intended for the names of works of art, may extend to character names in the event that they are used as title of a publication, or in cases where a character, because of its originality and memorability, is as well-known as a title character.[72] Unlike trade mark protection, the emergence of this title-protection is independent of registrations, and solely based on publication.[73] As trade marks in general, title protection grants protection against likelihood of confusion in the broadest sense. This includes any use, that may lead to the assumption of a commercial relationship.[74]

Alterations to a trade mark are to be treated according to Section 26 of the Trade Mark Act that implements Art 10 (1-2) lit a of the Trade Mark Directive. An alternate use of a trade mark, *i.e.* a use different from the way that the trade mark has been filed, fulfils the trade mark use requirement, as long as in the course of trade, the altered sign does not form a distinctive sign, different from the original trade mark.[75] This of course is essential to maintain the ability to base claims on the older registration date. The essential question is, whether the hypothetic consumer will recognize the original trade

---

70 Case C-206/01, Arsenal Football Club plc v. Matthew Reed, 2002 E.C.R. I-10273; Bundesgerichtshof [BGH] [Federal Court of Justice] Dec. 20, 2001, Gewerblicher Rechtsschutz und Urheberrecht [GRUR] 2002, 812 "Frühstücks-Drink II"; BGH Dec. 6, 2001, [GRUR] 2002, 814 "Festspielhaus"; BGH Dec. 5, 2002, [GRUR] 2003, 812, 332, 336 " Abschlussstück".

71 Ger. Trade Marks Act §§ 5, 15; Ger.: "Werktitelschutz".

72 Oberlandesgericht Hamburg [OLG Hamburg] [Higher Regional Court] Mar. 22, 2006, Gewerblicher Rechtsschutz und Urheberrecht – Rechtsprechungs-Report [GRUR-RR] 2006, 408 "OBELIX".

73 See supra note 55 § 15 at 260.

74 See supra note 8 at 7.4.1.4.

75 BGH May 31, 1975, GRUR 1975, 135; BGH June 20, 1984, GRUR 1984, 872 "Wurstmühle", BGH Apr. 17, 1986, GRUR 1986, 892 "Gaucho"; *see also* supra note 55 § 26 at 171.

mark as filed, when perceiving the altered sign.[76] Especially when taking into account the differences between the two signs, consumers should hold the two signs as equal. Insubstantial alterations, that is alterations that the public perceives as meaningless and exchangeable, are always to be considered maintaining the trade mark use.[77] This standard is practically identical to the one established by the GC in *Bainbrigde*, according to which "the sign used in trade differs from the form in which it is registered only in negligible elements so that the two signs can be regarded as broadly equivalent".[78]

In addition to the standard provided for by the Trade Mark Directive, Section 26 (3) adds that alterations that do not change the original character of the trade mark according to this doctrine are deemed to be use of the old trade marks, if the altered version as well has been registered.[79] That is to say trade mark owners who adapted their sign have the option of registering the new mark, without having to fear the loss of the old sign. This way, they can profit from the old mark's priority, while at the same time having the safety of a higher likelihood of protection upon the next modernization of the sign.

As the complex abovementioned standards for tolerable character adaptation let suspect, it is difficult to find a clear uniform criterion of to which extent changes are tolerable in existing case law. Also, it has to be kept in mind that this is a legal question that will be decided by courts on a case by case basis.[80] As to names, the change from "Jeanette" to "Jeannette" has been considered consistent with the

---

76 BGH Dec. 13, 2007, GRUR 2008, 714; BGH Feb 8, 2007, GRUR 2007, 592; BGH Jan 20, 2005, GRUR 2005, 515;BGH Aug 28, 2003, GRUR 2003, 1047 "Kellogg's/ Kelly's"; BGH Apr 13, 2000, GRUR 2001, 54 "SUBWAY/Subwear"; BGH Mar. 30, 2000, GRUR 2000, 1038; BGH Jul. 9 1998, GRUR 1999, 54; *see also supra* note 55 § 26 at 171.

77 Bundesgerichtshof [BGH] [Federal Court of Justice] July 13, 1979, Gewerblicher Rechtsschutz und Urheberrecht [GRUR] 1979, 856 "Flexiole"; BGH May 17, 1984 GRUR 1984, 813 "Ski-Delial"; BGH July 12, 1984 GRUR 1985, 46 "Idee Kaffee"; see also supra note 55 at § 26 Rn 171.

78 Case T-194/03, Il Ponte Finanzaria SpA v. OHIM et. al., 2006 E.C.R II-445 "Bainbridge"; aff'd in Case C-234/06, 2007 E.C.R. I-7333.

79 *See also supra* note 55 § 26 at 179.

80 *See supra* note 55 § 26 at 178.

original mark.[81] While no credible general prediction can be made, whether a complete overhaul or a modernisation of the graphic representation of a character will be consistent with the original mark, decisions concerning other non-conventional marks may provide some guidance. The coloration of a sign registered in black and white, without altering the sign's general impression has been be considered consistent with the registration,[82] especially in cases where coloration has become associated in the mind of a significant portion of the public.[83] The CJEU further elaborated its rationale that "by avoiding imposing a requirement for strict conformity between the form used in trade and the form in which the trade mark was registered,... [is] to allow the proprietor of the mark... to make variations in the sign, which, without altering its distinctive character, enable it to be better adapted to the marketing and promotion requirements of the goods or services concerned".[84] The addition of new features will likely be acceptable, if the new feature is an emphasis of a component already existing in the original sign.[85] The use of a different type of mark than the one registered will not be considered to be use of the original sign, e.g. the word mark "red line" is not in use by the mere application of red lines to a product.[86] Only for the sake of completeness it should be mentioned that infringement may subsist over the boundaries trade mark types.[87]

---

81 Bundespatentgericht [BPatG] [Federal Patent Court] Feb 14, 1995, Entscheidungen des Bundespatentgerichts [BPatGE] 35, 40 "Jeannette".
82 *See supra* note 55 § 26 at 199.
83 Case C-252/12, Specsavers Int'l Healthcare, Ltd. et. al. v. Asda Stores, Ltd., at 51 (Jul. 18, 2013) available at http://curia.europa.eu.
84 *Id.* at 29.
85 Bundespatentgericht [BPatG] [Federal Patent Court] Apr 11, 2000, Entscheidungen des Bundespatentgerichts [BPatGE] 43, 52 "COBRA BOSS".
86 Bundespatentgericht [BPatG] [Federal Patent Court] Feb. 16, 2000, 28 W (pat) 80/99 – *Application of a red line to goods is not use of the word mark "red line".*
87 Landgericht Köln [LG Köln] [Regional Court Cologne] Dec. 12, 2012, GRUR-RR 2013, 102; *prominently holding for dilution of the word mark "golden bear" by a product in the shape of a golden bear, "whose self-evident denomination amongst customers is identical with the word mark".*

2. Protection in the Community Trade Mark framework

While most of the above stated also applies under this chapter, some peculiarities of the Community Trade Mark system are to be pointed out. Although not expressly mentioned in the CTMR,[88] the OHIM requires applicants filing a Community Trade Mark to chose a mark category.

„The categorisation of marks serves a number of functions. Firstly, it establishes the legal requirement for the mark to be represented; secondly, it can help the examiner understand what the applicant is seeking to register; and finally, it facilitates research in the OHIM database."[89] Should the applicant fail to chose a mark type after a two month time limit set by the office, the examiner should choose the mark type he or she feels is appropriate.[90]

Marks particularly relevant for character protection include word marks for the name of the character, figurative marks and three-dimensional marks for its visual appearance and sound marks. As opposed to German sound marks, lingual components such as song-lyrics are eligible for registration,[91] as long as the fixation requirement is met. While CTMs, for the above mentioned reason are not apt to host complex personality traits, they may provide the means to protect certain behavioural patterns. For example a classic advertisement character testing the sensitivity of a toothbrush on a common tomato,[92] may be protected as a motion mark, described as: „The mark comprises a moving image consisting of a toothbrush moving towards a tomato, pressing onto the tomato without breaking the skin, and moving away from the tomato".

Like German law, Art. 15 CTMR allows for trade mark alterations that still constitute use of the unaltered sign, given that the distinctive

---

88 Commission Regulation EC No. 2868/95 of 13 December 1995, implementing Council regulation (EC) 40/94 on the Community Trade Mark O.J. (L 303).
89 OHIM – The Manual concerning Opposition: Examination of Formalities, Part B.2, at 8.
90 *Id.*
91 *Id.* at 8.4.
92 *See* CTM DR. BEST, Registration No. 9,742,974.

character of the trade mark is not altered. The GC further held that strict conformity between the sign as used and the sign registered is not necessary. However, the difference must be in negligible elements and the signs as used and registered must be broadly equivalent.[93] In order to decide whether this broad equivalence is fulfilled, courts will first establish which elements of the mark are negligible, and which are dominant, further verifying whether the dominant elements are still present in the altered mark.[94] The General Court has held that „the assessment of the distinctive or dominant character of one or more components of a complex trade mark must be based on the intrinsic qualities of each of those components, as well as on the relative position of the different components within the arrangement of the trade mark".[95] Additions and omissions of dominant elements of the mark will likely result in discontinuity.[96] The public perception will not be taken into account.[97]

The results seem fairly casuistic, holding against continuity when abbreviating the name „Tony Hawk" to „Tony"[98] while holding for continuity in the case of „BIFI" despite dramatic changes in colour and typeface and the omission of a hyphen in the middle of the word.[99]

---

93 Case T-194/03, Bainbridge 2006 E.C.R II-445 para 50. *See also supra* note 78.

94 See also OAMI The Manual Concerning Opposition, Part 6 – Proof of use at 7.3.

95 Case T-135/04 GfK AG v. OHIM, 2005 E.C.R. II-04865 "Online Bus" para 36.

96 *Id. See also* case T-353/07 Esber SA v. OHIM, 2009 E.C.R. II-226 "Coloris" paras 29 et seq., case T-482/08 Atlas Transport v. OHIM 2010 E.C.R. II-108 paras 36 et seq.

97 See supra note 93.

98 OHIM Opposition division, Quicksilver, Inc. v. Exori Import- Export GmbH & Co. KG, Ruling on Opposition B 1,034,208 (Oct. 14, 2008), *available at* http://oami.europa.eu/LegalDocs/Opposition/2008/en/001034208.pdf.

99 OHIM First Board of Appeal, Unilever N.V. v. Kaiku Corporacion Alimentaria, S.L., Case R 0877/2009-1, (April 29, 2010) *available at* http://oami.europa.eu/LegalDocs/BoA/2009/en/R0877_2009-1.pdf.

B. Copyright

Germany

Copyright protects an author's "own intellectual creation in the literary, scientific and artistic domain"[100] for 70 years after the author's death.[101] General requirement for the protection under the German Copyright Act is that the work meets a minimum threshold[102] of originality – in the sense of a minimum degree of individuality, or a sufficient degree of creative originality[103] of the work[104] – to award copyright protection. While characters are not explicitly mentioned as a category of work under of the German Copyright Act,[105] their protection under several categories of works has been historically recognized. Even though the extent of originality actually needed under the German Copyright Act is disputed[106] and somewhat fuzzy, characters are prone to be more complex than the average works of authorship, thus likely to meet this requirement. The CJEU's recent tendency to take a very liberal approach to subject matter eligible for copyright protection further fortifies character protection under copyright law.[107]

Graphic representations may qualify as works of visual arts under Section 2 (1) Nr. 4 G.C.A.Besides to the individual expression of works of literature, the German copyright system also awards protection to the "fable", meaning the course of action in the work and

---

100 Gesetz über Urheberrecht und Verwandte Schutzrechte – Urbheberrechtsgesetz [UrhG][Copyright Act], Sept. 9, 1965 Bundesgesetzblatt [BGBl] S. 1273 as amended, § 2.
101 *Id.* § 65 et. seq.
102 Ger.: "Schöpfungshöhe".
103 Bundesgerichtshof [BGH] [Federal Court of Justice] Dec. 10, 1987, Gewerblicher Rechtsschutz und Urheberrecht [GRUR] 1988, 533 at 535.
104 Thomas Dreier & Gernot Schulze, Urheberrechtsgesetz: UrhG, (4th ed., 2013) § 2 at 20 et seq.
105 Copyright Act § 2.
106 *See supra* note *104* § 2 at 21.
107 Cf. Case C-5/08 Infopaq Int'l A/S v. Danske Dagblades Forening 2009 E.C.R. I-6569; Case C-393/09 Bezpečnostní softwarová asociace v. Ministerstvo kultury 2010 E.C.R. I- 13971 "BSA".

its arrangement,[108] which may cover certain behavioural patterns of characters.[109]

Furthermore, courts have granted copyright protection to characters per se in a number of cases where these characters fulfilled the above mentioned criteria for protection, and were personally imprinted elements determining the form of the original work, in which they appeared.[110]

As early as 1958, the BGH has awarded copyright protection to a visually depicted character beyond its concrete fixed expression, taking into account visual character features that were capable of implying the presence of certain personality traits.[111] The BGH further elaborated this doctrine in a second decision concerning the same character, stating "the protection extends to an anthropomorphic hedgehog-figure with original physiognomy, whose characteristic visual features make the impression of a personality, that in its core has a mischievous yet sweet-natured hedgehog-personality".[112] In 1984, the Higher Regional Court Frankfurt followed the BGH, extending to entire categories of characters by holding (in a slightly more technical wording): "The Smurf is to be awarded copyright protection".[113] However the BGH seemed to apply a somewhat contradictory approach to infringement analysis in his "Sherlock Holmes" decision, stating that no infringement could be found in cases where only the visual appearance of a character was imitated, without actually imitating the character in question.[114] The graphic representation thus

---

108 *Id.* § 24 at 22.
109 Ralph Graef, *Die fiktive Figur im Urheberrecht* [*The Fictitious Character in Copyright Law*], Zeitschrift für Urheber- und Medienrecht [ZUM] 2012, 108 at 109 (2012).
110 *Id.* at 111.
111 Bundesgerichtshof [BGH] [Federal Court of Justice] Apr. 1, 1958, Gewerblicher Rechtsschutz und Urheberrecht [GRUR] 1958, 500 "Mecki-Igel".
112 Bundesgerichtshof [BGH] [Federal Court of Justice] Dec. 8, 1959, Gewerblicher Rechtsschutz und Urheberrecht [GRUR] 1960 251, 252 "Mecki II".
113 OLG Frankfurt am Main [OLG FFM] [Higher Regional Court Frankfurt am Main] Feb. 23, 1984, Gewerblicher Rechtsschutz und Urheberrecht [GRUR] 1984, 520 "Schlümpfe".
114 Bundesgerichtshof [BGH] [Federal Court of Justice] Nov. 15, 1957, Gewerblicher Rechtsschutz und Urheberrecht [GRUR] 1958, 54 "Sherlock Holmes".

was being used as yardstick for copyright protection of a character, but was not subject of copyright protection.

In 1993, the BGH first formulated an impartial test to determine whether a character was protected by copyright or not,[115] demanding "a characteristic and unmistakeable combination of external qualities such as personality traits, skills and typical behavioural patterns".[116] Consequently, several courts acknowledged the copyright protection for Astrid Lindgren's classic Figure "Pipi Longstocking",[117] partially deviating from the Sherlock Holmes doctrine by granting protection to Pipi's flamboyant visual appearance per se.[118]

To determine whether a character is infringing older character rights[119] or whether it is covered by the "free use exception",[120] the conceptual distance between the old work and the new work is decisive. For this purpose, courts have adapted[121] the "fading doctrine",[122] according to which free use is granted only in cases where the content taken from the older work protected by copyright is being reduced to a role so marginal, that the old work fades to a weak and irrelevant state in the context of the new work.[123] Hence, a work can be considered "fair use", if it is a complete new creation that was merely inspired by the original work.[124] Decisive in this context are the correlations between the two works, not the differences.[125] The stronger and more distinct the original character is, the larger is its

---

115 *See also* supra note 109 at 111.

116 BGH Mar. 11, 1993, GRUR 1994, 191 at 192 "Asterix-Persiflagen".

117 Landgericht Hamburg [LG Hamburg] [Regional Court Hamburg] Apr. 28, 2009, ZUM 2009, 581; Landgericht Berlin [LG Berlin] [Regional Court Berlin] Aug. 11, 2009 ZUM 2010, 69; Oberlandesgericht Köln [OLG Köln] [Higher Regional Court Köln] Oct. 14, 2011, 6 U 128/11 *available at* http://justiz.nrw.de.

118 Landgericht Kiel [LG Kiel] [Regional Court Kiel], Apr. 28, 2011, 15 O 22/11, *available at* Beck online.

119 § 23 German Copyright Act.

120 § 24 German Copyright Act.

121 *See supra* note 116 at 193.

122 Ger.: "Verblassens-Formel".

123 Friedrich Fromm & Wilhelm Nordemann, Urheberrecht (10 ed. 2008) § 24 UrhG at 3.

124 *See supra* note 104 § 24 at 8.

125 *See also* supra note 109 at 114.

scope of protection.[126] However, in a recent decision on claimed infringement of a literary character by selling a carnival costume with resemblances to that character, the BGH held that even when a mental connection to a very distinctive characters is being created, mere allusions or the reception of minor elements from a character do not automatically rule out free use.[127]

Exceptions to this rule exist for cases of parody, in which the BGH tends to apply a less stringent standard, and is more likely to decide for free use.[128] Despite the fact that German copyright law does not allow for free assignability of works, the possibility to grant user rights, leading to a de facto assignment of rights, degrades this fact to a mere contracting problem.[129]

C. Unfair Competition Law

Germany

The unauthorized use of a trade mark, and the unauthorized use of another undertaking's commercial indicator – including characters[130] – may qualify as anticompetitive hindrance[131] under Section 4, para. 10 of the German Unfair Competition Act.[132] This may result from

---

126 *Id.*
127 Press release, BGH, Urheberrechtlicher Schutz einer literarischen Firgur [Copyright Protection of a Literary Character] (concerning the unpublished judgement BGH July 17, 2013, I ZR 52/12), *available at* http://juris.bundesgerichtshof.de; *see also* BGH Mar. 11, 1993 GRUR 1994, 206 "Alcolix"; contra supra note 109 at 116.
128 *See supra* note 121 at 198.
129 *Id.* at 131.
130 Annette Kur, *Der wettbewerbliche Leistungsschutz – Gedanken zum wettbewerbsrechtlichen Schutz von Formgebungen, bekannten Marken und "Characters"* [*Protection under Competition Law – Thoughts on the Protection of Shapes, Famous Marks and Characters*], GRUR 1990, 1, 5.
131 Wolfgang Gloy, Michael Losschelder & Willi Edelmann, Handbuch des Wettbewerbsrechts § 56 IV at 91 (4 ed. 2010); Michael Enzinger, Lauterkeitsrecht at 415 et. seq. (2012), *with a comparison to the legal situation in Austria.*
132 Gesetz gegen den unlauteren Wettbewerb [UWG] [Unfair Competition Act], May 27, 1896, Bundesgesetzblatt [BGBl] I S 254, as amended.

imitation,[133] exploitation of goodwill,[134] or the "approach" to a well-known trade mark.[135] Anticompetitive hindrance may materialise in the endangerment of valuable signs by direct competitor, non-competitor, and in the protection of a secured legal position arising from the prior use of a sign.[136]

In general, the protection under the U.C.A. is subsidiary to trade mark protection.[137] Unfair competition protection thus applies only in cases, where the requirements for trade mark infringement are not met, most notably in the rare cases where the imitator is not using the sign as a trade mark.[138]

The protection of a secured legal position arising from the prior use of a sign is intended to cover cases, in which an undertaking used a certain sign in commerce, without acquiring trade mark protection for it. Due to the strict first to register system, a second comer could acquire a registration and highjack the mark on grounds of trade mark infringement.[139] Given that the first adopter has acquired a valuable interest in the sign, in the sense of a significant degree of market recognition, and given that the sign has acquired goodwill amongst the target group of the product the sign is used for, the enforcement of a later registered identical or confusingly similar trade mark can be fenced off on grounds of competition law. This exception to the strict registration requirement only applies, if the latter registrant was acting knowingly of the earlier sign, and is subject to a case-by-case decision, taking into account all the extent and intensity of all circumstances having impact on competition.

While this may seem like a very vague and weak form unregistered trade mark protection, it may bear substantial advantages in the protection of advertisement characters inherent to registration based trade

---

133 BGH Dec 10, 1986, GRUR 1987, 903 at 905 "Le Courboisier Möbel".
134 BGH Nov 8, 1984, GRUR 1985, 876 at 878 "Tchibo/Rolex".
135 BGH Nov 29, 1999, GRUR 1991, 465 "Salomon"; BGH Dec 6, 1990, GRUR 1991, 609 "SL"; BGH Feb 10, 1994, GRUR 1994, 808 "Markenverunglimpfung".
136 *See supra* note 131 at 92.
137 *See supra* note 131 at 93.
138 *See supra* chapter III.A.1.
139 *See supra* note 131 at 97.

mark systems. Features that require the proof of acquired distinctiveness are not eligible for trade mark protection right away. If such features deviate from the overall commercial expression of the mark, they exceed its scope, thus resulting in a "gap of protection" between the first adoption of the feature, and the acquisition of distinctiveness. Based on unfair competition law, mark owners are supplied with a possibility to bridge this gap of protection.[140]

Precondition for protection against "endangerment of signs" is that the sign has acquired a "high degree of fame or a particular prestige value and reputation", embodying "a high, value to the owner, created by his own effort". This is relevant especially in cases, where marketing characters are subject to libel by a competitor, but not used as a trade mark.

D. Other forms of protection

Protection via personality rights?

Under the German legal system, personality rights protect manifold elements encompassed by real persons, most notably a person's name, voice and image. Unlike the U.S., there is no distinction between the right to privacy and the right to publicity – personality rights are inalienable and can not be subject to licensing in the closer meaning of the word. While it is thinkable that the voice of a fictitious character overlaps with the voice of an individual, thus being protected under personality rights,[141] no case involving this scenario has been reported yet.

The Austrian legal system however, following an approach to personality protection very similar to that of Germany, has had a high profile supreme court case.[142] "MA2412" a popular television programme about the allegedly legendary laziness of Austrian public

---

140 *See supra* chapter III.A.1.
141 Or more precisely: the right to one's voice.
142 Oberster Gerichtshof [OGH] [Supreme Court] Mar. 20, 2003, docket No, 6 Ob 270/01a, *available at* http://ris.bka.gv.at (Austria).

servants, featured its principal characters talking in strongly exagger-
ated accents, and highly over-pitched voices. When imitations of these
voice were used in a radio commercial, the actors sought to enjoin the
use of "their" voices on grounds of personality protection. The Austrian Supreme Court affirmed the decision for the plaintiffs. Some
commentators praised this decision as a fast and efficient way of en-
forcing the right to one's voice,[143] all despite fact, that it was not the
actors' voices that were imitated, but much rather the characters'.[144]

---

143 *See supra* note 25.
144 *See also* Feldman *supra* note 3 at 709.

IV. United States of America

A. The federal trade mark system

1. Protection of characters[145]

While the main functions of federal U.S. trade mark law are the subject of scholarly discussion, the most common purposes are seen in:[146] (1) allowing for the identification of a seller's goods and services and the distinction from a competitor's goods or services; (2) signifying that all goods and services bearing the mark stem from an identical commercial source (3) signifying the equal quality of the goods bearing the mark and (4) serving as an instrument in advertising and selling goods.

While the trade mark protection of a character per se, or the establishment of a property right in a character, is not possible, protection may arise if a character also serves as an indicator of origin.[147]

The most obvious difference to the German system is that adoption of marks is based on actual use of the sign. Activities that constitute use include not only the use in a trade mark manner,[148] but also "anal-

---

145 *See generally*: J. Thomas McCarthy, McCarthy on Trademarks and Unfair Competition (4 ed. 2013); Jerome Gilson, Gilson on Trademarks (Lexis Nexis 2013); Louis Altman & Mara Pollack, Callman on Unfair Competition, Trademarks and Monopolies (Thomson Reuthers 2013); David Hilliard, Joseph Welch & Uli Widmaier, Trademarks and Unfair Competition (8 ed. 2010).

146 *See* McCarthy *supra* note 145 § 3:1 at 104.

147 Ex parte Carter Publications 92 U.S.P.Q. (BNA) 251 (Comm'r Pat. & Trademarks 1952); In re: Circus Foods, Inc., 252 F.2d 310 (C.C.P.A. 1958); Peter Shapiro, *The Validity of Registered Trademarks for Titles and Characters After the Expiration of Copyright on the Underlying Work*, 31 COPYRIGHT L. SYMP. (ASCAP) 69, 88-89; Pillsbury Co. v. Milky Way Prods. 215 U.S.P.Q. (BNA) 124 (N.D. Ga. 1981); Jantzen Knitting Mills v. Spokane Knitting Mills Inc., 44 F.2d 656 (D. Wash 1930); Helfland supra note 20 at 634. *See also*: In re DC Comics, 689 F.2d 1042 (C.C.P.A. 1982).

148 Microstrategy, Inc. v. Motorola, Inc, 245 F.3d 335 at (4th Cir. 2001) 341 et seq.

ogous use" (meaning: as a designator of origin other than one affixed directly on the product, or displayed in close proximity of the goods),[149] if such use has "substantial impact on the purchasing public".[150] The option to file for a mark based on the bona fide "intent to use",[151] does not award the applicant a position equal to a mark holder,[152] thus not changing the fundamental requirement of actual use. U.S. trade marks offer protection from use of the same mark or "colorable imitations"[153] of it, meaning imitations, likely to cause confusion or mistake or to deceive.[154] In practice, likelihood of confusion is based on a multi-factor test, taking into account a variety of elements.[155] While the duration of trade mark protection is theoretically perpetual, the scope of protection is limited to "use in commerce".[156] This term, however is to be interpreted rather broadly.[157] Furthermore, federal trade marks are protected from the likelihood of dilution by tarnishment or blurring.[158]

As stated above, the emergence of trade mark protection by actual use of the sign in commerce is the decisive criterion to enforce a mark.[159] As opposed to the German approach to unfair competition law, considering it as a legal category independent and different from trade mark law, in the U.S. trade mark law and unfair competition law are interwoven, or as one may put it "thread of the same cloth".[160]

---

149   15 U.S.C. § 1127 (2006). See also: Persha v. Amour & Co., 239 F.2d 628 (5th Cir. 1957).
150   T.A.B. Systems v. PacTel Teletrac, 77 F.3d 1372 (Fed. Cir. 1996) at 1375.
151   Trademark Law Revision Act of 1988, Pub. L. No. 100-667, Stat 3935 (Nov 16, 1989) amending 15 U.S.C. 1051 et. seq.
152   Zazu Designs v. L'Oreal, S.A., 979 F.2d 499, 504 (7th Cir. 1992).
153   15 U.S.C. § 1114 (2006).
154   *Id.*
155   *See e.g.* Judge Friendly in Polaroid Corp. v. Polarad Electronics Corp., 287 F.2d 492, 495 (2d Cir. 1961).
156   15 U.S.C. § 1114 (2006).
157   15 U.S.C. § 1127 (2006); *cf.* Rescuecom, Corp. v. Google, Inc. 562 F.3d 123, 127 (2nd Cir. 2009).
158   15 U.S.C. § 1125 as amended by the Trademark Dilution Revision Act (2006) H.R. 683; *statutorily rejecting* Moseley v. V Secret Catalogue, Inc. 537 U.S. 418 (2003).
159   *See* Hanover Star Milling Co. v. Metcalf 240 U.S. 403 (1916).
160   This image is credited to the legal scholar and practitioner Paul Geller.

Lanham Act § 43(a)[161] codifies unfair competition on the federal level, prohibiting among other things the use of any word, term, name, symbol, or device, or any combination thereof, or any false or misleading designations of origin, descriptions or representation that is likely to cause confusion as to origin. Given the high degree of similarity, courts apply trade mark rules such as the multi-factor test for likelihood of confusion[162] for substantive purposes.[163] Thus, it represents a claim for infringement of non-registered marks equivalent to registered marks.[164] This puts owners of character trade marks in the comfortable position of basing claims on character aspects that have been registered, and such that have not been registered cumulatively. In conclusion, both can be treated under the same chapter.

As early as 1921,[165] in the "Mutt and Jeff" case, courts have recognized characters' ability to act as such an indicator, and have held that the creator of characters "is the owner of the proprietary right existing in the characters"[166] under trade mark law. However early decisions recognized this right only in as far as it was vested in the name and visual appearance of the characters.

The advent of the Lanham Act[167] introduced an even more liberal regime in terms of subject matter eligible for trade mark protection, defining the term trade mark as "any word, name, symbol, or design, or any combination thereof, used in commerce to identify and distinguish the goods of one manufacturer or seller from those of another and to indicate the source of the goods."[168] While characters per se are not expressly mentioned as a trade mark category, they are covered

---

161 15 U.S.C. § 1125 (2006).
162 *See supra* note 153.
163 *See supra* note 161.
164 Banff Ltd v. Federated Dep't Stores, Inc., 841 F.2d 486 (2d Cir. N.Y. 1988); A.J. Canfield Co. v. Honickman 808 F.2d 291, 296 (3d Cir. Pa. 1986); Union Mfg. Co. v. Han Baek Trading Co. 763 F.2d 42, 47-48 (2d Cir. N.Y. 1985).
165 Harry C. Fisher v. Star Company 231 N.Y. 414, 132 N.E. 133, cert denied 257 U.S. 654 (N.Y. 1921) Widely known as the "Mutt and Jeff" decision after the Characters in question.
166 Fisher v. Star Co. 231 N.Y. 414, 425 (1921).
167 15 U.S.C. § 1051 (2002) et. seq.
168 15. U.S.C. § 1127 (2006).

by the broad wording and definition applied by the Lanham Act,[169] and have been found to be able to act as a trade mark.[170]

The line between protection of a character itself and the protection of the artist impersonating the character is fuzzy. In Oliveira v. Frito-Lay Inc.,[171] the singer of the famous song "The Girl from Ipanema" tried to prevent a foods manufacturer from using this song in an advertisement on grounds of trade mark law. Despite the plaintiff's arguments that she "had become known as the girl from Ipanema" herself,[172] and hence was acting as the fictional character that was to be protected, the court dismissed the claims for trade mark infringement. This is not to be interpreted as a bar to trade mark protection for characters, considering that in this case "The Girl from Ipanema" was much rather a nickname of the artist than a character, lacking development of substantial character traits and not being enacted by the plaintiff, but rather besung from meta level.

As illustrated above by the "Mutt and Jeff" case, a character's name and its visual appearance have long been acknowledged to be able to serve as trade marks under the types of "words and images". In this respect, following general trade mark mechanics, the mark owner need not necessarily show the acquisition of secondary meaning, but may gain protection based on the inherent distinctiveness of these aspects.[173] Protection has been awarded against the use of the character itself[174] as well as the mere allusion to a character.[175]

---

169 *See* McCarthy *supra* note 145 § 7 at 105. *See also e.g.* Qualitex Co. v. Jacobson Products Co. 514 U.S. 159, 162 (1995).

170 Fisher v. Star Co. 231 N.Y. 414; *see also* Franklin Waldheim, *Mickey Mouse – Trademark or Copyright,* 54 Trademark Rep. 865, 869 (1964).

171 Oliveira v. Frito-Lay, 251 F.3d 56 (2nd Cir. 2001).

172 *Id.* at 59.

173 See McCarthy supra note 145 § 10 at 42; But cf. Supra note 165.

174 Walt Disney Co. v. Powell, 698 F. Supp. 10 (D.D.C 1988); Universal City Studios, Inc. v. J.A.R. SALES, Inc., 216 U.S.P.Q. 679 (C.D. Cal 1982); Patten v. Superior Talking Pictures, 8 F. Supp. 196 (D.C.N.Y. 1934); Toho Co., Ltd. v. William Morrow and Company, Inc., 33 F. Supp. 2d 1206 (C.D. Cal 1998), *based on the word mark "GODZILLA".*

175 Conan Properties; Inc. v. Conans Pizza, Inc., 752 F.2d 145 (5th Cir. 1985).

The protectability of other, more sophisticated aspects of characters physical abilities or personality traits has been denied by courts[176] with varying justifications. In CBS v. DeCosta, the court held that characters were eligible for no protection beyond copyright.[177] In DC v. Filmation the court based his decision on the consideration that "Plaintiff has cited no case and we have found none, holding that physical abilities or personality traits are protectable under § 43 (a) of the Lanham Act", and that the protection of character traits "more properly lies under the copyright act."[178]

I find this argumentation hardly convincing, considering that the broad wording of the Lanham Act, and the legal practice of allowing the registration of particular shapes and sounds, as long as they are able to "carry meaning",[179] and thus are apt to serve as a source identifier.[180] In cases where personality traits are well developed and characteristic of a character, this will easily be the case. The objection that a personality trait, unlike a shape or a sound can not be described or delineated precisely enough is unconvincing, as the U.S. system, unlike the German system, does not require a strict uniformity of signs to serve as trade marks. The Plumeria blossom case, in which protection was granted to an olfactory mark, very vaguely described as "a high impact, fresh, floral fragrance reminiscent of plumeria blossoms"[181] serves as a prime example for the legality of marks, that are not precisely delineated under the U.S. System.[182] On a side-note, personality traits and similar qualities of spokes-characters, unlike

---

176 Columbia Broadcasting System, Inc. v. DeCosta, 377 F.2d 315 (1st Cir. 1967); DC Comics, Inc. v. Filmation Associates, 486 F.Supp. 1273 (S.D.N.Y. 1980); see also McCarthy supra note 145 § 10 at 42, citing the the apparently unrelated decision 77 U.S.P.Q.2D (BNA) 1220.

177 *Contra:* Coca-Cola Co. v. Rodriguez Flavouring Syrups Inc., 89 U.S.P.Q. 36 (Chief Examiner 1951); *see generally* McCarty supra note 145 § 6 at 31.

178 *See supra* note 176 *DC v. Filmation* 486 F.Supp. at 1277.

179 *See* Qualitex 514 U.S. 159, 162.

180 15 U.S.C. § 1127; William Landes & Richard Posner, *The Economics of Trademark Law,* 78 Trademark Rep. 267, 290 (1988).

181 In re Celia Clarke 17 U.S.P.Q.2d (BNA) 1238, 1238 (T.T.A.B. 1990).

182 *See also*: "A cherry scent" Reg. No. 2,463,044; "The Strawberry Scent of the Goods" Reg. No. 2,596,156; "The scent of bubble gum" Reg. No. 2,560,618; "The Scent of Grapes" Reg. No. 2,568,512.

most colour or shape marks,[183] will be construed as a source identifier by consumers, thus being inherently distinctive.

This of course, calls for strict purposive delineation to copyright law, e.g. by applying a stricter notion of trade mark use. In Comedy III Productions, Inc v. New Line Cinema,[184] the owner of all rights and interests in the three Stooges attempted to fence off the use of a short film sequence from a Three Stooges movie in the background of another movie on grounds of trade mark protection. While the court held that the sequence in question was not protected under trade mark law, it more notably added that the defendant did not use the movie extract as a "commercial vehicle", hence was not using it as a trade mark.[185] Courts however seem to deviate from this strict approach, adopting a more rights-holder friendly position vis-à-vis infringement: In a case of human rights activists adopting the name of a character for their street patrol,[186] the District Court for the Southern district of New York held for trade mark infringement based on likelihood of confusion, "despite" the fact that the character in question was supposedly famous.[187] Commentators have concluded, that "When the mark is a character ... courts appear more likely to find confusion, even if the defendant's work is an obvious parody".[188]

The need for such protection is evident in scenarios, in which a mental connection to a competitor's product is constructed by copying that competitor's marketing character's personality while staying clear of said character's name or visual appearance. This holds true even for advertisement characters whose dominant feature is an intangible one, like their sense of humour or their accent. Furthermore, evidence in the USPTO-register suggests that there is actual need for the protection of personality traits, in order to effectively protect advertisement characters, especially spokes-characters. Right holders have

---

183 *See* Qualitex 514 U.S. 159, 163.
184 Comedy III Productions Inc v. New Line Cinema, 200 F.3d 593 (4th Cir. 1999).
185 *Id.* at 596.
186 MGM-Pathe Communications Co. v. The Pink Panther Patrol, 774 F.Supp. 869 (S.D. N.Y. 1991).
187 *Id.* at 874.
188 See supra note 20 at 661.

tried working around legal limitations and register character traits per se in creative ways. In order to protect the undisputed Star of their 2010 Superbowl commercial, a bouquet of anthropomorphic, wilted mail-order flowers yelling insults at their unsuspecting recipient,[189] the owner registered a sound mark, described as "The mark consists of sounds of men and women laughing and making mocking, derisive or sarcastic comments"[190] The USPTO held this description to be too vague,[191] and required additional details, which ultimately lead to the abandonment of the mark. The Jolly Green Giant, whose laughter can be considered his sole personality trait met a similar fate, when its registration was abandoned.[192] The Pillsbury doughboy, with his characteristic giggle still active on the registry, seems to lonely stand his ground.[193] In addition to that, protection may arise as a side effect of the registration of more general features, such as the registration of sales techniques or the overall look and feel of the branding as trade dress.[194] However, as opposed to the name and visual appearance of a character, this will require the proof of secondary meaning.[195]

The appeal of characters makes them a prime object of merchandising, leading to constellations in which the ornamental qualities of a character constitutes the major value the product. The sale of bulk items such as t-shirts, may generate substantially higher revenue when fitted with the depiction of a popular character. Copyright ownership of characters in use for entertainment typically triggers trade mark ownership in characters and secondary meaning,[196] as consequence

---

189 *Cf.* Teleflora Superbowl Commercial (Aug. 24, 2013 4:50 PM) https://www.youtube.com/watch?v=Oy0UN7OI-cg.

190 WILTED FLOWERS, Registration No. 77,621,516 (abandoned Mar 2 2010).

191 *See* U.S.P.T.O. Registration No. 77/621516 office action Feb 9th 2009.

192 THE JOLLY GREEN GIANT'S LAUGH, Registration No. 75,821,499 (cancelled Sept 19, 2008).

193 POPPIN' FRESH'S GIGGLE, Registration No. 76,163,189.

194 Philip Morris Inc. v. Star Tobacco Corp., 879 F. Supp 379 at 383 (S.D.N.Y. 1995), *resulting in protection for the "Marlboro Man" as side effect of the registration of the general advertisement theme of the Marlboro brand.*

195 Wal-Mart Stores, Inc. v. Samara Brothers, Inc. 529 U.S. 205 (2000).

196 Universal City Studios 216 U.S.P.Q. At 682; Disney v. Powell 698 F. Supp. 10 at 12; DC Comics. v. Filmation Associates 486 F. Supp. 1273 at 1276 et seq.; Fleischer Studios Inc. v. A.V.E.L.A, Inc. 772 F.Supp. 2d 1155 at 1168 (C.D.Cal 2009).

of uninterupted, exclusive use. This leads to the problematic situation where owners of characters created primarily for entertainment, and not marketing purposes, acquire trade mark protection, gaining a wider scope of protection based on the dilution doctrine. This can lead to a de facto perpetuation of their copyrights in the character, rendering the copyright bargain useless.[197] The question, whether the owner of a character may resort to trade mark protection to enjoin unauthorized merchandising use is disputed. Practitioners and trade mark owners have argued that trade mark protection in merchandising is a *fait accompli* based on economic realities, justifying this approach with the unfairness of free-riding on investments made in developing the character.[198] Scholars have remained critical towards this approach,[199] arguing that an investment-based approach to trade mark protection inherently leads to difficulties when finding the limits to protection. In order for each of the doctrines to appropriately serve their economic purpose, a balance has to be struck between copyright and trade mark protection and their economic purposes. "If trade mark law is reduced to ensuring a return on producer investment, it will be difficult to establish limits on its reach. If the consumer-regarding aspects of trade mark law are given prominence, it may become easier to reconcile trade mark law to one role and copyright law to another."[200] In Boston Hockey, judicial practice[201] has opened the door to character protection via trade mark law by introducing the doctrine of likelihood of association, according to which even in the absence of actual consumer confusion the creation of an association to a mark constitutes trade mark infringement. Congress[202] has later provided for a statutory regulation, by amending Section 43 (a) of the Lanham

---

197 *See also:* Lee Burgunder, *The Scoop on Betty Boop: A Proposal to Limit Over-reaching Trademarks,* 32 Loy. L.A. Ent. L. Rev. 257 (2011-2012).
198 Irene Calboli, *The Case for a Limited Protection of Trademark Merchandising,* 2011 U. Ill. L. Rev. 865, 887 (2011).
199 Robert G. Bone, *Enforcement Costs and Trademark Puzzles,* 90 Va. L. Rev. 2099, 2111 (2004); *See also supra* note 198 at 886 *et. seq.*
200 Dinwoodie *supra* note 53 at 520.
201 Boston Hockey 510 F.2d 1004, *supra* note 26.
202 *See* S. Rep. No. 100-515, at 4 (1988).

Act to include mistake or deceiption "as to origin, sponsorship or approval" as infringing behaviour.

In its Dastar[203] decision, the U.S. Supreme court relativised its formerly liberal approach on the scope of trade mark protection. In this case, the plaintiff was the copyright owner of a television series that had fallen into the public domain. The defendant had edited the television series and sold it as his own product, without making reference to the plaintiff. The court held against the plaintiff's claim based on reverse passing off, by having made a false designation of origin. The crucial question essentially being whether the term "origin" as used in Section 43 (a) Lanham Act refers only to the source that made the product available to the public or manufacturing it, or also to the source of the underlying work.[204] The Court held for the former, stating that the latter *"would create a species of mutant copyright law that limits the public's "federal right to copy and to use" expired copyrights."*[205] Some commentators have argued that this reasoning is to be understood as construing a definite bar on merchandising based on trade mark law,[206] since merchandisers are the source of the underlying work and not the product itself. This however does not take into account, that merchandising will not incorporate a "designation of origin", but much rather a term, name, symbol or device, thus not being part of Dastar's ratio decidendi. The decision thus offers only a minor relieve against the problem of perpetuation.

In its recent "Betty Boop" decision,[207] the Ninth Circuit revisited the problem of perpetuation, by applying the criterion of aesthetic functionality to the defendant's merchandising use of the mark and holding such use to be non-infringing. While this controversial decision has been withdrawn by the court, it nevertheless refueled the discussion about the ability to acquire trade mark protection for characters, and the potential danger of perpetuation of copyrights. Also,

---

203 Dastar Corp. v. Twentieth Century Fox Film Corp. 539 U.S. 23(2003).
204 *Id.* at 35.
205 *See* Dastar v. Fox 539 U.S. 23, 34 [*citations omitted*].
206 Cf. Jennifer Konefal, *Federal Trademark Law in an Uncertain State*, 11 B.U. J. Sci. & Tech. L. 283 (2005).
207 Fleischer Studios Inc. v. A.V.E.L.A, Inc. 772 F.Supp. 2D 1155 (9th Cir 2011).

it implied that trade mark protection in character merchandising is not as firmly entrenched as trade mark owners and practitioners may suggest.

Some commentators have argued[208] that a more stringent application of the aesthetic functionality doctrine may provide a solution to this problem. Comparing the aesthetic quality characters add to a movie with that a colour adds to a piece of garment, a case can be made against the protection of characters. This of course, will not affect characters created merely for the purpose of advertisement, that fulfil trade marks economic purpose.[209] *Burgunder* suggested a primary purpose test, awarding trade mark protection based on the initial purpose the character was created for.[210]

However, it seems doubtful whether this proposition is realistically workable, not only because of the high administrative cost involved, but also because a delineation of a sign's purpose can not always be made. There are grey zones, in which characters partially act as designator of origin but in the meantime add entertainment or other substantial value to a product. Furthermore, it is thinkable, that a symbol's role evolves from purely ornamental one, to that of a designator of origin. If the Disney Company should decide to enter the garment business, Mickey Mouse may well evolve into a designator of origin. A clear delineation where a sign has ceased serving its original entertainment purpose, and has turned into a designator of origin can hardly be made. More importantly, applying the criterion of aesthetic functionality – isolated from its original purpose of emergence of a mark – to questions of infringement seems dogmatically displaced.

As already implied by the Court in the original Betty Boop decision,[211] the problem at hand is more elegantly solved by deviating from the likelihood of association doctrine, focussing on consumer protection and applying the trade mark use doctrine. Following traditional trade mark mechanics, character merchandising, when limi-

---

208 *See generally supra* note 215.
209 *Id.* at 289.
210 *Id.*
211 Fleischer v. A.V.E.L.A 772 F.Supp. 2D 1155.

ted to the sheer application of a character's counterfeit to a bulk article, is not to be considered trade mark use, but merely as copyright use.[212] As it has been so concisely put by Lord Bridge of Harwich in an analogous U.K. case: "Character Merchandising deceives nobody [...] Nobody who buys a Mickey Mouse shirt supposes that the quality of the shirt owes anything to Walt Disney productions".[213] Should however, the use of the sign change in a way, that it can be considered a designator of origin, e.g. by diversification into the fashion industry, there is no reason why the eligibility for trade mark protection should be barred on grounds of aesthetic functionality. By setting the limits of trade mark subject matter by notions of distinctiveness,[214] a balance can be struck between trade mark and copyright.

This leads to the difficult problem of delineation, when the merchandising use of a character can be considered trade mark use. Some commentators have suggested[215] to judge trade mark use based on the number and combination of marks visible on the final product. This, however, seems like a generalization that may not be practicable in all industries. While clothing labels may be interpreted as designators of origin by large parts of the public, and images of characters printed on the fabric in addition to the label be construed as purely ornamental, modern marketing often creates situations that are more complex and elusive. The use of characters in television commercials in combination with conventional branding come to mind. A more practicable solution would be to give judges leeway in decision-making in the form of a flexible system, with which the economic purpose of the character use can be grasped.[216]

---

212 *See* Waldheim *supra* note 170 at 867.
213 *See* Holly Hobbie Trade Mark, (1984) 329 R.P.C. (H. L.) (UK).
214 *Cf.* Dinwoodie *supra* note 53 at 502.
215 Anne-Virginie Gaide, Copyright, Trademarks and Trade Dress: Overlap or Conflict for Cartoon Characters?, Proceedings of the ALAI Congress, June 13-17, 2001, 560 *et seq.*
216 *Cf.* Waldheim *supra* note 170 at 867.

2. Adaptation of trade marks

In general, marks may be protected even after they have been subject to modernizations or alterations. To assess the protection of altered or modernized marks, courts rely on the "commercial impression" rule. In general, mark owners will be able to claim the original mark's priority for an altered mark, if it creates the same commercial impression as the original mark.[217] The mark owner is therefore entitled base claims on the priority of the initial sign. If however, the mark is altered to an extent that continuity of the commercial impression is not maintained by the altered sign, the modification will be considered as abandonment of the old sign.[218] Lead by the Federal Circuit, courts later have clarified that the similarity needed is greater than mere likelihood of confusion, requiring the "same continuing commercial impression test requires a greater, albeit undefined degree of similarity … making tacking on the old mark's priority only admissible in the rare cases where the old and new formats are legal equivalents",[219] "either indistinguishable or virtually identical".[220] Courts apply this commercial impression test in an increasingly stringent manner, denying continuity even in cases of multiple word marks, in which only a single, generic word was changed,[221] or denying an owner priority who changed his fairly simple logo from a "rounded" to a more "angular" design.[222] In terms of characters, this strict approach will limit protection only to cases where the character is slightly modernized in order to transport an ageing character into the present, or to increase

---

217 Hess's of Allenton, Inc. v. National Bellas Hess, Inc, 169 U.S.P.Q. (BNA) 673 at 687 (T.T.A.B. 1971); Ilco Corporation v. Ideal Security Hardware Corporation, 527 F.2d 1221 at 1224 (C.C.P.A. 1976); *see also supra* note 145 McCarthy § 17 at 26.

218 *See supra* note 145 Hilliard, Welch, Widmaier § 4.03 at B-4.

219 *See* McCarthy supra note 217; Van Dyne-Crotty, Inc. v. Wear-Guard Corp., 926 F. 2d 1156, (Fed. Cir. 1991).

220 One Industries, LLC v. Jim O'Neal Distributing Inc., 578 F.3d 1154 at 1161 (9ᵗʰ Cir. 2009).

221 See: American Paging Inc. v. American Mobilephone, Inc. 13 U.S.P.Q.2d (BNA) 2036 (T.T.A.B. 1989), aff'd 923 F.2d 869, 17 U.S.P.Q. 1726 (Fed Cir. 1990), holding against continuous commercial impression between the word marks "AMERICAN MOBILEPHONE" and "AMERICAN MOBILEPHONE PAGING".

222 One v. Jim O'Neal, 578 F.3d 1154 at 1161.

the character's commercial impact. This will be a likely scenario in cases where the strive for continuity and sensibility towards the marks original image (hence: the connection to the goodwill) is a common goal of lawyers and designers alike.[223] Any change more substantial to the character, such as the alteration or adding of features, will not be protected under the "commercial impression rule" thus possibly constituting a new mark.

B. Copyright

The federal Copyright Act of 1976,[224] awards protection to works that display a minimum degree of originality and fulfil the fixation requirement. Originality in this sense is already acquired when the work is independently created and possesses a minimum degree of creativity.[225] While spokes-characters are created for the purpose of distinguishing the origin of goods and services, and their creation therefore arguably requires no incentive through copyright protection, they will in practically all cases be able to fulfil these requirements.

Works that are subject to copyright protection include literary works, musical works, dramatic works, pictorial and graphic works and motion pictures as well as other audiovisual works.[226] The fact that characters are not expressly covered by the scope of copyright protection, has made some commentators express the need for the introduction of such category into copyright law.[227] Courts however have worked around this lack of express mention in the law by awarding protection to characters as copyrightable components of preexisting works.[228]

---

223 See also: Beverly Pattishall, *The Goose and the Golden Egg – Some Comments about Trademark Modernization*, 47 Trademark Rep. 801 (1957).
224 Copyright Act of 1976 17 U.S.C. §§ 101-810 (2010).
225 Feist Publications, Inc. v. Rural Tel. Service, 499 U.S. 340 (1991).
226 17 U.S.C. § 102 (a) (2010).
227 *See also* Feldman *supra* note 3 at 687.
228 17 U.S.C. § 103 (2010).

Copyright grants its owner the exclusive right to reproduce his work and to prepare derivative works based on the copyrighted work as well as to publicly perform and publicly display the work.[229] In general, protection is being awarded independent of the way, the character was initially fixed. Courts have held three dimensional characters to be infringing works that were fixed in a two dimensional manner.[230] Furthermore, protection was granted outside the context in which characters initially occurred,[231] and independent of the medium in which they were originally fixed.[232]

This protection is substantially limited by two legal mechanisms. Firstly, the Copyright Act of 1976 inherently limits the scope of protection by explicitly mentioning the idea/expression-dichotomy: "In no case does copyright protection for an original work of authorship extend to any idea, procedure, process, system, method of operation, concept, principle, or discovery, regardless of the form in which it is described, explained, illustrated, or embodied in such work".[233]

In addition to that, exclusive rights conferred by the Copyright Act are subject to the limitations of the fair use doctrine, according to which copyrighted works may be copied "for purposes of such as criticism, comment, news reporting, teaching,... scholarship without infringing the copyright.[234] Courts use a flexible system in determining whether a use is to be considered fair or not, primarily taking into account among other factors the purpose and character of the use, the nature of the work, the substantiality of the portion used in relation to the entire work, its effect on the market of the used work and the intent of the person copying.[235] These interests are weighed against the legitimate interests of the author. As far as character protection is concerned, fair use will most likely be granted for parody,[236] which, de-

---

229 17 U.S.C. § 106 (2010).
230 Ideal Toys Corp. v. Kenner Products, 443 F. Supp 291 (S.D.N.Y. 1977).
231 United Artists vs. Ford Motor Co., 483 F. Supp. 89 (S.D.N.Y. 1980).
232 Burroughs v. Metro-Goldwyn-Mayer Inc., 683 F.2d 610 (2d Cir. 1982).
233 17 U.S.C. § 102 (b) (2010).
234 17 U.S.C. § 107 (2010).
235 17 U.S.C: § 107 (2010).
236 *See also* Helfland, supra note 20, at 631.

pending on the circumstances may also be given in commercial uses.

The emergence and extent of character's copyright protection has been subject of manifold court rulings, thus having evolved significantly over time. Noteworthy is the fact that courts apply different standards to purely literary characters, and characters with a physical embodiment, such as a pictorial representation, a fact that is considered ironic by some, since literal character are often more sophisticated than "mere cartoons" or even sketches.[237]

Nichols v. Universal Pictures Corp opened the door to copyright protection of literary characters, but Judge Learned Hand did so only under careful observance of the limits inherent in the idea/expression-dichotomy.[238] Learned Hand reasoned that "It follows that the less developed the characters, the less they can be copyrighted; that is the penalty an author must bear for making them too indistinctly".[239] Based on this reasoning, the two-step "well-developed character" test was established as the standard criterion for copyright infringement in characters, firstly inquiring whether the character has been sufficiently delineated, and secondly analysing substantial similarity between the allegedly infringing character and the original character.[240] As to the detail needed for a character to be considered "well-developed", case law seems inhomogeneous: While Judge Learned Hand apparently had a fairly sophisticated standard in mind,[241] later courts awarded copyright protection for characters as developed as "Tarzan is the ape-man. He is an individual closely in tune with his jungle environment, able to communicate with animals yet able to experience human emotions. He is athletic, innocent youthful gentle

---

237 *See supra* note 20 at 631, *see also* Leslie Kurtz, *The Independent Legal Lives of Fictional Characters*, 1986 Wis. L. Rev 429, 472 (1986); *See generally* Feldman *supra* note 3.

238 Nichols v. Universal Pictures Corp., 45 F.2d. 119 (2d Cir. 1930).

239 *Id.* at 121.

240 *See supra* note 20 at 631, *see also supra* Feldman in note 3 at 691.

241 *See supra* note 238 at 121.

and strong".[242] Whether the deciding court has ever heard of Rudyard Kipling's "Jungle Book" has not been conveyed.

A stricter reasoning was implemented in the "Sam Spade" case.[243] The starting point of this case was the question whether the transfer of rights to an entire novel leads to the transfer of rights to the characters featured in the novel as well.[244] Elaborating the "well-developed character" doctrine, the court held that the "if the character is only the chessman in the game of telling the story he is not within the area of protection afforded by the copyright",[245] hence not subject to the transfer of rights.

In contrast to this stringent standard to protect literary characters, protection was more easily obtainable for characters with physical embodiment. This becomes most evident when analysing early cases concerning conflicting comic characters. In Detective Comics, Inc. v. Bruns Publications[246] for example, the court held the defendant's character "Wonderman" to be infringing the plaintiff's "Superman", despite the latter being characterized by little more than being "a man of miraculous strength and speed... dressed in a skintight acrobatic costume",[247] "with the ability of being impervious to bullets",[248] thus not being outstandingly well developed by the standards of *Nichols*.[249] Albeit the court did not intend to award "a monopoly to the mere character of a 'superman' who is a blessing to mankind",[250] the extent of protection granted indicates a rather lackadaisical application of the idea/expression dichotomy.[251] Quintessentially, "Superman" was awarded Copyright protection, despite being of higher sim-

---

242　*See supra* note 232 at 622-623.

243　Warner Bros. Pictures, Inc. v. Columbia Broadcasting Sys., 216 F.2d 945 (9th Cir. 1954).

244　*Id. See also* Feldman *supra* note 3 at 693, Timothy Anderson v. Sylvester Stallone 11 U.S.P.Q.2d (BNA) 1161 (C.D. Cal 1989).

245　Warner Bros 216 F.2d at 950.

246　Detective Comics, Inc. v. Bruns Publications, Inc. 111 F.2d 432 (S.D.N.Y. 1940).

247　*Id.* at 433.

248　*Id.*

249　*See supra* note 238 at 121.

250　*See supra* note 246 at 434.

251　*See also supra* note 20, at 634.

plicity than the average literary character. This holding was later restricted in National Comics Publications v. Fawcett Publications,[252] clarifying it is to protect only "specific exploits of 'Superman' as each picture portrayed them", arguably a major restriction to the extent of protection[253] and a re-approach to the classic idea/expression dichotomy.[254]

However, these criteria were later loosened by the introduction of what should become known as the "look and feel test",[255] awarding protection not merely for specific exploits of a character, but to the more abstract "combination of many different elements which may command copyright protection because of its particular subjective quality".[256] The court held that where "characters each have developed personalities and particular ways of interacting with one another and their environment",[257] the protection awarded by copyright exceeds the specific exploits. Framing this approach in the terminology used in Sam Spade, protection is awarded to the story being told, unless the characters of the story exceed the role of a "mere chess man",[258] and the characters themselves constitute the story being told.[259]

This approach was entrenched by the Ninth Circuit's affirmation of Disney vs. Air Pirates,[260] ruling "a character (as opposed to the work in which it appears) is protectable, if it is 'especially distinctive' such that it has widely 'identifiable traits'."[261] The court limited the application of this doctrine to characters with graphical representations,

---

252 National Comics Publ'n, Inc. v. Fawcett Publ'n, Inc., 191 F.2d 594 (2d Cir. 1951).

253 *Supra* note 20, at 634.

254 *See also* Feldman *supra* note 3 at 694.

255 Sid & Marty Krofft Television Productions v. McDonald's Corp. 562 F.2d 1157 (9th Cir. 1977).

256 *Id.* at 1169.

257 *Id.*

258 *See supra* note 243 at 950.

259 Walt Disney Productions v. The AIR PIRATES et al., 345 F. Supp. 108 at 113 (N.D. Cal 1972), *aff'd in part and rev'd in part by* 581 F.2d 751. (9th Cir. 1978).

260 *Id.*

261 *Id.* at 755-756. *See also* Toho 33 F. Supp. 2d at 1216; Metro-Goldwyn-Mayer, Inc. v. Am. Honda Corp., 900 F. Supp. 1287, 1297 (C.D. Cal 1995).

reasoning that "which has physical as well as conceptual qualities, is more likely to contain some unique elements of expression".[262] It should be mentioned that by taking into account the distinctiveness of the character in question, and the "widespread recognition of the characters involved",[263] the court seemed to be partially applying trade mark law rationale in a copyright analysis. This doctrinal convergence of copyright and trade mark law has been criticised by some commentators.[264]

Another requirement of character protectability is that of consistent depiction. In Walker v. Viacom International, Inc.[265] the court held that apart from the lack of distinctiveness of the plaintiff's character "Bob Spongee", it was inconsistently portrayed in comic strips and advertisements. This lack of consistency ultimately defeated the plaintiff's claim that the stand-alone character ... is protected".[266] In terms of character adaptations, courts tend to award protection despite inconsistent depiction, in cases where characters have developed a "constant set of traits".[267] While the addition of new features triggers a new period of copyright protection in those features, it will not grant further protection beyond the alteration's original embellishments and additions to the underlying character.[268] This is sensible, for minor amendments should not serve as a strategy to prolong character protection.

D. Other forms of protection

In Groucho Marx Productions v. Day and Night Co.[269] the court applied the right of publicity to protect a fictional character, by ruling

---

262 *Id.* at 755. *see also* Feldman in supra note 3 at 694.
263 *Id.* at 757.
264 *See generally supra* note 20 at 644 et seq.
265 Troy Walker v. Viacom International, Inc., No. C 06-4931 SI, 2008 U.S. Dist. LEXIS 38882, *see also* Rice v. Fox Broad Co. 330 F.3d 1170, 1175 (9th Cir. 2003).
266 *Id.* at 16.
267 As was the case for "Godzilla" Toho 33 F. Supp. 2d at 1216.
268 Harvey Cartoons v. Columbia Pictures Indus. 645 F.Supp. 1564 (S.D.N.Y. 1986).
269 Groucho Marx Prods. v. Day & Night Co., 523 F. Supp. 485 (S.D.N.Y. 1981).

that "the defendants have ... reproduced (the plaintiff's) manner of performances by imitating their style and appearance" and stating this was an infringement of the plaintiff's right to publicity.[270] This is however inconsistent with the traditional U.S. approach to publicity protection, applying to the commercial exploitation of a real person and not a fictitious character.[271] Commentators have judged the court's decision as outright erroneous, stating "In this case the court confused the creators with their characterizations, and, consequently, misapplied the right of publicity to the latter. The defendant's play did not appropriate the actors themselves, only their characters."[272]

However, there is one overlap between publicity rights and personality traits that has been recognized by courts. In cases of voice misappropriation, the imitation of the voice of a fictitious character may at the same time be an infringement of the publicity rights of the human voice artist, thus can be enjoined on this legal basis.[273]

While this may lead to situations in which a change in the voice artist results in the new voice artist infringing the old one's right to publicity, this will not result in an alteration of the character, thus not being in the scope of this paper.

---

270 *Id.* at 492-493.
271 *See* Feldman *supra* note 3 at 709.
272 *Id.*
273 Lahr v. Adell Chem. Co., 300 F.2d 256 (1ˢᵗ Cir. 1962); Booth v. Colgate-Palmolive Company 362 F. Supp. 343 (S.D.N.Y. 1973).

V. Synthesis, conclusion and policy recommendations

Many of the aspects that constitute a character, especially its name, its physical appearance and its signature phrases are covered by trade mark law in Germany and the United States alike. This allows for a potentially perpetual regime of protection from confusingly similar uses, supplemented by even more extensive protection through the doctrine of dilution, and recent CJEU jurisdiction on double identity. Infringement does not necessitate direct copying, but will regularly only given in cases where the infringing sign is used in commerce.

Character modernizations and alterations are only tolerable to a minimal extent, as the modernised character must create a continuous commercial impression. This will usually be given in cases of "natural" character development – as in the conventional evolution all characters, fictitious or not, undergo – but not necessarily in cases where characters are overhauled to comply with altered market demands. While it is undoubted that under certain circumstances intangible character features such as personality traits are able to act as designators of origin no more or less than other nonconventional trade marks, courts and trade mark offices alike seem reluctant to grant protection for opaque reasons. While the German and European approach is dogmatically more convincing, by basing its aloofness on the principle of the uniformity of the trade mark, U.S. courts' mere reference to Copyright as a more appropriate regime seems inconsistent with general trade mark law mechanics, and even more so with the regime concerning non-conventional trade marks. However, the industry's strong reliance on these characters, and manifold registration attempts on the registers prove, that there is demand for said protection. Considering the fact that characters created for advertisement purposes pass the test of serving their purpose as designators of origin with flying colours – especially in comparison with other non-conventional marks, and further given the fact that the characters in question are consistent with the economical rationale behind trade mark law, a strong case can be made for a doctrinal pivot towards a more appreciative regime.

While U.S. unfair competition law in principle serves the same purpose as trade mark law, German unfair competition law only provides for the very basic protection of unregistered signs in hardship cases.

Copyright has traditionally been the native regime for the protection of characters, and serves as a strong alternative to trade mark law by taking a traditionally holistic approach to character protection, referring to the entire character rather than its isolated features. In light of the above described gaps in trade mark protection, character owners will, in most cases, be able to resort to copyright protection in order to protect their characters. Since the protection is not dependent on any formalities, this flexibility allows for the automatic protection of character modernisations and alterations. Protection is, however, limited in duration. While the extent of the duration will likely be sufficient for the majority of all characters, there have been, and will be further cases of characters outliving their copyright protection. In cases of spokes-characters, that were initially created to serve as designators of origin, the limited term of copyright protection will prevent efficient and sustainable protection of aspects not eligible for trade mark protection.

Despite the fact characters are constructed analogously to human beings, and possess a similar pattern of assets and features, protection granted under the rights to personality, privacy or publicity can be considered as side-notes or mere curiosities.

Finally, as far as character merchandising is concerned, the problem of perpetuation of copyrights via trade mark law seems entrenched in the system. Deriving from opportunistic lawyering and short-sighted jurisprudence, despite ongoing critique by scholars, the enforcement of character merchandising by means of trade mark law – regardless of its economic rationale – has become a commonplace phenomenon. Furthermore, merchandising has developed into a fully-fledged industry, generating substantial revenues. However, as recent court rulings suggest that this return-on-investment based rationale is being rethought by U.S. courts. The situation calls for a clear statutory solution of this dilemma most elegantly and thus preferably by means of adaptation of the trade mark use requirement – clearly stating that merchandising is not considered to be use as a trade mark. The alleged status quo, granting extended protection to copyright owners causes deadweight loss, and is harming the public interest. The need for such a change in jurisprudence thus is evident.

Semantically, the case for a stricter trade mark use requirement is a clear-cut one. Character merchandising, by its nature, is merely ornamental. Merchandising does not allow for distinction as to origin of a product it is applied to, and therefore is not a trade mark use. Economically, there is no sensible reason to grant perpetual protection for characters, that do not serve the public interest by acting as a designator of origin.

Characters are protected under the copyright regime for a considerable duration already, leaving no need for the further incentivization of their creation. Granting trade mark protection for merchandising uses would extend this monopoly even further, without causing any additional benefit for the general public.

If a character is actually used as a trade mark – regardless of the question whether it was created for marketing purposes, or whether the character was created for entertainment, and later used as a designator of origin – it is likely to serve its distinctive purpose better than conventional signs, and thus deserves the same degree of protection. A distinction after the purpose of the character at the time of its creation does not sufficiently take this into account.

While trade mark owners that actually use their signs as designators of origin, or use it only for certain goods and services, would not be impaired, merchandisers could reap the benefits of their characters for the duration of their copyright protection.

List of works cited

I. National Statutes

1. United States of America

Lanham (Trademark) Act, 15 U.S.C. §§ 1051 et seq. (2013).

Trademark Law Revision Act of 1988, Pub. L. No. 100-667, Stat 3935 (Nov 16, 1989) amending 15 U.S.C. 1051 et. seq.

U.S. Copyright Act, 17 U.S.C. §§ 101 et seq. (2013).

2. European Union

a) Community Statutes

Directive 2008/95/EC, of the European Parliament and the Council af 22 October 2008 to approximate the Laws of the Member States Relating to Trade Marks, O.J. (L 299) 25 – "Trade Mark Directive".

Commission Regulation EC No. 2868/95 of 13 December 1995, implementing Council regulation (EC) 40/94 on the Community Trade Mark O.J. (L 303).

b) Austria

Markenschutzgesetz 1970, BGBl 1970/260 idF 2009/126 (Austrian Trademark Act) (2013).

Bundesgesetz über das Urheberrecht an Werken der Literatur und der Kunst und über verwandte Schutzrechte – Urheberrechtsgesetz, BGBl 111/1936 idF 2010/58 (Austrian Copyright Act) (2013).

c) Germany

Gesetz über den Schutz von Marken und sonstigen Kennzeichen – Markengesetz [MarkenG] [Trade Marks Act], Oct. 25, 1994 Bundesgesetzblatt [BGBl] I S. 3082 as amended.

Gesetz über Urheberrecht und Verwandte Schutzrechte – Urbheberrechtsgesetz [UrhG] [Copyright Act], Sept. 9, 1965 Bundesgesetzblatt [BGBl] S. 1273 as amended.

Gesetz gegen den unlauteren Wettbewerb [UWG] [Unfair Competition Act], May 27, 1896, Bundesgesetzblatt [BGBl] I S 254, as amended.

II. Court Rulings and other decisions

1. United States of America

A.J. Canfield Co. v. Honickman 808 F.2d 291, 296 (3d Cir. 1986).

American Paging Inc. v. American Mobilephone, Inc. 13 U.S.P.Q.2d (BNA) 2036 (T.T.A.B. 1989), aff'd 923 F.2d 869, 17 U.S.P.Q. 1726 (Fed Cir. 1990).

Banff Ltd v. Federated Dep't Stores, Inc., 841 F.2d 486 (2d Cir. 1988).

Bonito Boats, Inc. v. Thunder Craft Boats, Inc. 489 U.S. 141 (1989).

Booth v. Colgate-Palmolive Company 362 F. Supp. 343 (S.D.N.Y. 1973).

Boston Professional Hockey Association, Inc. v. Dallas Cap & Emblem Mfg., Inc. 510 F.2d 1004 (5th. Cir. 1975).

Burroughs v. Metro-Goldwyn-Mayer Inc., 683 F.2d 610 (2d Cir. 1982).

Ex parte Carter Publications 92 U.S.P.Q. (BNA) 251 (Comm'r Pat. & Trademarks 1952).

In re: Circus Foods, Inc., 252 F.2d 310 (C.C.P.A. 1958).

In re Celia Clarke 17 U.S.P.Q.2d (BNA) 1238 (T.T.A.B. 1990).

Coca-Cola Co. v. Rodriguez Flavouring Syrups Inc., 89 U.S.P.Q. 36 (Chief Examiner 1951).

Columbia Broadcasting System, Inc. v. DeCosta, 377 F.2d 315 (1st Cir. 1967).

Comedy III Productions, Inc v. New Line Cinema, 200 F.3d 593 (4th Cir. 1999).

Conan Properties; Inc. v. Conans Pizza, Inc., 752 F.2d 145 (5th Cir. 1985).

Dastar Corp. v. Twentieth Century Fox Film Corp. 539 U.S. 23 (2003).

In re DC Comics, 689 F.2d 1042 (C.C.P.A. 1982).

DC Comics, Inc. v. Filmation Associates, 486 F.Supp. 1273 (S.D.N.Y. 1980).

Detective Comics, Inc. v. Bruns Publications, Inc. 111 F.2d 432 (S.D.N.Y. 1940).

E. Wine Corp. v. Winslow-Warren, Ltd. 137 F.2d 955 (2d Cir. 1943).

Feist Publications, Inc. v. Rural Tel. Service, 499 U.S. 340 (1991).
Fleischer Studios Inc. v. A.V.E.L.A, Inc. 772 F.Supp. 2d 1155 (9th Cir 2011).

Groucho Marx Prods. v. Day & Night Co., 523 F. Supp. 485 (S.D.N.Y. 1981).

Hanover Star Milling Co. v. Metcalf 240 U.S. 403 (1916).
Harry C. Fisher v. Star Company 231 N.Y. 414, 132 N.E. 133, cert denied 257 U.S. 654 (N.Y. 1921).
Harvey Cartoons v. Columbia Pictures Indus. 645 F.Supp. 1564 (S.D.N.Y. 1986).
Hess's of Allenton, Inc. v. National Bellas Hess, Inc., 169 U.S.P.Q. (BNA) 673 (1971).

Ideal Toys Corp. v. Kenner Products, 443 F. Supp 291 (S.D.N.Y. 1977).
Ilco Corporation v. Ideal Security Hardware Corporation, 527 F.2d 1221 (1976).

Jantzen Knitting Mills v. Spokane Knitting Mills Inc., 44 F.2d 656 (D. Wash 1930).

Lahr v. Adell Chem. Co., 300 F.2d 256 (1st Cir. 1962).

Metro-Goldwyn-Mayer, Inc. v. Am. Honda Corp., 900 F. Supp. 1287, (C.D. Cal 1995).
MGM-Pathe Communications Co. v. The Pink Panther Patrol, 774 F.Supp. 869 (S.D. N.Y. 1991).
Microstrategy, Inc. v. Motorola, Inc, 245 F.3d 335 at (4th Cir. 2001).
Moseley v. V Secret Catalogue, Inc. 537 U.S. 418 (2003).

National Comics Publ'n, Inc. v. Fawcett Publ'n, Inc., 191 F.2d 594 (2d Cir. 1951).
Nichols v. Universal Pictures Corporation, 45 F.2d 119 (1930).

Oliveira v. Frito-Lay, 251 F.3d 56 (2nd Cir. 2001).
One Industries, LLC v. Jim O'Neal Distributing Inc., 578 F.3d 1154 (9th Cir. 2009).

In re: Nuclear Research Corporation, 16 U.S.P.Q.2D (BNA) 1316 (1990).

Persha v. Amour & Co., 239 F.2d 628 (5th Cir. 1957).
Philip Morris Inc. v. Star Tobacco Corp., 879 F. Supp 379 (S.D.N.Y. 1995)
Pillsbury Co. v. Milky Way Prods. 215 U.S.P.Q. (BNA) 124 (N.D. Ga. 1981).
Polaroid Corp. v. Polarad Electronics Corp., 287 F.2d 492, 495 (2d Cir. 1961).
Prestonettes, Inc. v. COTY, 264 U.S. 359 (1924).

Qualitex Co. v. Jacobson Products Co. 514 U.S. 159 (1995).

Rescuecom, Corp. v. Google, Inc. 562 F.3d 123 (2nd Cir. 2009).
Rice v. Fox Broad Co. 330 F.3d 1170 (9th Cir. 2003).

Sid & Marty Krofft Television Productions v. McDonald's Corp. 562 F.2d 1157 (9th Cir. 1977).

T.A.B. Systems v. PacTel Teletrac, 77 F.3d 1372 (Fed. Cir. 1996).

Timothy Anderson v. Sylvester Stallone 11 U.S.P.Q.2d (BNA) 1161 (C.D. Cal 1989).

Toho Co., Ltd. v. William Morrow and Company, Inc., 33 F. Supp. 2d 1206 (C.D. Cal 1998).

TrafFix Devices, Inc. v. Mktg. Displays Inc., 532 U.S. 23, 34 (2001).

Troy Walker v. Viacom International, Inc., No. C 06-4931 SI, 2008 U.S. Dist. LEXIS 38882.

Union Mfg. Co. v. Han Baek Trading Co. 763 F.2d 42, 47-48 (2d Cir. 1985).

United Artists vs. Ford Motor Co., 483 F. Supp. 89 (S.D.N.Y. 1980).

Universal City Studios, Inc. v. J.A.R. SALES, Inc., 216 U.S.P.Q. 679 (C.D. Cal 1982).

Patten v. Superior Talking Pictures, 8 F. Supp. 196 (D.C.N.Y. 1934).

Van Dyne-Crotty, Inc. v. Wear-Guard Corp., 926 F.2d 1156, (Fed. Cir. 1991).

Wal-Mart Stores, Inc. v. Samara Brothers, Inc. 529 U.S. 205 (2000).

Walker v. Viacom International, Inc. No. C 06-4931 SI, 2008 U.S. Dist. LEXIS 38882 (2008).

Walt Disney Co. v. Powell, 698 F. Supp. 10 (D.C.C. 1988).

Walt Disney Productions v. The AIR PIRATES et. al., 345 F.Supp. 108 (1972).

Warner Bros. Pictures, Inc. v. Columbia Broadcasting Sys., 216 F.2d 945 (9th Cir. 1954).

Zazu Designs v. L'Oreal, S.A., 979 F.2d 499, 504 (7th Cir. 1992).

2. European Union

Case C-206/01, Arsenal Football Club plc v. Matthew Reed, 2002 E.C.R. I-10273.

Case C-393/09 Bezpečnostní softwarová asociace v. Ministerstvo kultury 2010 E.C.R. I- 13971.

Case C-102/77, Hoffmann-La Roche & Co., AG et. al v. Centrapharm Vertriebsge-sellschaft Pharmazeutischer Erzeugnisse, m.b.H. 1978 E.C.R. 1139.

Case C-234/06, Il Ponte Finanzaria SpA v. OHIM et. al., 2007 E.C.R. I-7333.

Case C-5/08 Infopaq Int'l A/S v. Danske Dagblades Forening 2009 E.C.R. I-6569.

Case C-299/99, Koninklijke Philips Electronics NV v. Remington Consumer Products Ltd., 2002 E.C.R. I-5475.

Case C-104/01, Libertel Groep BV v. Benelux Merkenbureau 2003 E.C.R. I-3793.

Case C-487/07, L'Oréal SA et. al. v. Bellure NV et. al. 2009 E.C.R. I-5185.

Case C-273/00, Ralf Sieckmann v. Deutsches Patent- und Markenamt, 2002 E.C.R. I-11737.

Case C-283/01, Shield Mark BV v. Joost Kist 2003 E.C.R. I-14313.

Case C-252/12, Specsavers Int'l Healthcare, Ltd. et. al. v. Asda Stores, Ltd. Jul. 18, 2013; available at http://curia.europa.eu.

Case T-482/08 Atlas Transport v. OHIM 2010 E.C.R. II-108.

Case T-353/07 Esber SA v. OHIM, 2009 E.C.R. II-226 "Coloris".

Case T-135/04 GfK AG v. OHIM, 2005 E.C.R. II-04865.

Case T-194/03, Il Ponte Finanzaria SpA v. OHIM et. al., 2006 E.C.R II-445.

3. Great Britain

Holly Hobbie Trade Mark, (1984) 329 R.P.C. (H. L.).

4. Germany

BGH Dec. 13, 2007, GRUR 2008, 714.

BGH Feb 8, 2007, GRUR 2007, 592.

BGH Jan 20, 2005, GRUR 2005, 515.

BGH Aug 28, 2003, GRUR 2003, 1047 "Kellogg's/Kelly's".

BGH Dec. 5, 2002, GRUR 2003, 812 "Abschlussstück".

BGH Dec. 20, 2001, GRUR 2002, 812 "Frühstücks-Drink II".

BGH Dec. 6, 2001, GRUR 2002, 814 "Festspielhaus".

BGH Apr 13, 2000, GRUR 2001, 54 "SUBWAY/Subwear".

BGH Mar. 30, 2000, GRUR 2000, 1038.

BGH Jul. 9 1998, GRUR 1999, 54.

BGH Mar. 11, 1993, GRUR 1994, 191 "Asterix-Persiflagen".

BGH Dec. 10, 1987 GRUR 1988, 533.

BGH Apr. 17, 1986, GRUR 1986, 892 "Gaucho".

BGH July 12, 1984 GRUR 1985, 46 "Idee Kaffee"

BGH June 20, 1984, GRUR 1984, 872 "Wurstmühle".

BGH May 17, 1984 GRUR 1984, 813 "Ski-Delial"

BGH July 13, 1979, GRUR 1979, 856 "Flexiole".

BGH May 31, 1975, GRUR 1975, 135.

BGH Dec. 8, 1959, GRUR 1960 251 "Mecki II".

BGH Apr. 1, 1958, GRUR 1958, 500 "Mecki-Igel".

BGH Nov. 15, 1957, GRUR 1958, 54 "Sherlock Holmes".

Press release, BGH, Urheberrechtlicher Schutz einer literarischen Firgur [Copyright Protection of a Literary Character] (concerning the unpublished judgement BGH July 17, 2013, I ZR 52/12), *available at* http://juris.bundesgerichtshof.de.

BPatG Apr 11, 2000, BPatGE 43 "COBRA BOSS".

BPatG Feb. 16, 2000, 28 W (pat) 80/99.

BPatG Feb 14, 1995, BPatGE 35 "Jeannette".

OLG Köln Oct. 14, 2011, 6 U 128/11.

OLG Hamburg Mar. 22, 2006, GRUR-RR 2006, 408 "OBELIX".

OLG Frankfurt am Main Feb. 23, 1984 GRUR 1984, 520 "Schlümpfe".

LG Kiel Apr. 28, 2011, 15 O 22/11.

LG Köln Dec. 12, 2012, GRUR-RR 2013, 102.

LG Hamburg Apr. 28, 2009, ZUM 2009, 581.

LG Berlin Aug. 11, 2009 ZUM 2010, 69.

5. Austria

OGH Mar. 20, 2003, docket No., 6 Ob 270/01a, *available at* http://ris.bka.gv.at.

6. International law

Paris Convention for the Protection of Industrial Property Art. 5, Mar. 20, 1883, 21 U.S.T. 1583, 828 U.N.T.S. 305.

III. Journal Articles/Reports

1. United States of America

Robert G. Bone, *Enforcement Costs and Trademark Puzzles*, 90 Va. L. Rev. 2099 (2004).

Ralph Brown, *Advertising and the Public Interest, Legal Protection of Trade Symbols*, 57 Yale L.J. 1206 (1948).

E. Fulton Brylawski, *Protection of Characters – Sam Spade revisited*, 22 Bull. Copyright Soc'y 77 (1974).

Lee Burgunder, *The Scoop on Betty Boop: A Proposal to Limit Overreaching Trademarks*, 32 Loy. L.A. Ent. L. Rev. 257 (2011-2012).

Lee Burgunder, *Trademark Registration of Product Colours: Issues and Answers*, 26 Santa Clara L.Rev. 581 (1986).

Irene Calboli, *The Case for a Limited Protection of Trademark Merchandising*, 2011 U. Ill. L. Rev. 865 (2011).

Graeme Dinwoodie, *Trademark and Copyright: Complements or Competitors?*, Proceedings of the ALAI Congress, June 13-17, 2001.

Giselle Fahimian, *How the IP Guerrillas Won: Trademark, Adbusters, Negativeland, and the "Bullying Back" of Creative Freedom and Social Commentary*, 2004 Stan. Tech. L. Rev. 1 (2004).

David B. Feldman, *Finding a Home for Fictional Characters: A Proposal for Change in Copyright Protection*, 78 Calif. L. Rev. 687 (1990).

Anne-Virginie Gaide, Copyright, Trademarks and Trade Dress: Overlap or Conflict for Cartoon Characters?, Proceedings of the ALAI Congress, June 13-17, 2001.

Judith Garretson & Roland Niedrich, *Spokes-Characters – Creating Character Trust and Positive Brand Attitudes*, Journal of Advertising, volume 33, no. 2 (2004), 25-36.

Benjamin A. Goldberger, *How the "Summer of the Spinoff" Came to be: The Branding of Characters in American Mass Media*, 23 Loy. L.A. Ent. L. Rev. 301 (2003).

Paul Goldstein, *The Competitive Mandate: From Sears to Lear*, 59 Cal. L. Rev. 873 (1971).

Michael Todd Helfland, *When Mickey Mouse Is as Strong as Superman: The Convergence of Intellectual Property Laws to Protect Fictional Literary and Pictorial Characters*, 44 Stan. L. Rev. 623 (1992).

Jennifer Konefal, *Federal Trademark Law in an Uncertain State*, 11 B.U. J. Sci. & Tech. L. 283 (2005).

Leslie Kurtz, *The Independent Legal Lives of Fictional Characters*, 1986 Wis. L. Rev 429 (1986).

William Landes & Richard Posner, *The Economics of Trademark Law,* 78 Trademark Rep. 267, 290 (1988).

Jessica Litman, *Breakfast with Batman: The Public Interest in the Advertising Age*, 108 Yale L. J. 1717 (1999).

Michael V. P. Marks, *The Legal rights of Fictional Characters,* 25 Copyright L. Symp. (ASCAP) 35 (1980).

Beverly W. Pattishall, *The Goose and the Egg – Some Comments about Trademark Modernization*, 47 Trademark Rep. 801 (1957)

Peter Shapiro, *The Validity of Registered Trademarks for Titles and Characters After the Expiration of Copyright on the Underlying Work*, 31 Copyright L. Symp. (ASCAP) 69.

Preet K. Tummala, *The Seinfeld Aptitude Test: An Analysis Under Substantial Similarity and the Fair Use Defense*, 33 U.C. Davis L. Rev. 289 (1999).

Franklin Waldheim, *Mickey Mouse – Trademark or Copyright*, 54 Trademark Rep. 865, (1964).

2. European Union

Manoranjan Ayilyath, Character Merchandising and Personality Merchandising: The Need for Protection – An Analysis in the Light of UK & Indian Laws, Entertainment Law Review (Sweet & Maxwell, London) 23- 3 (2012).

Ralph Graef, Die fiktive Figur im Urheberrecht [The Fictitious Character in Copyright Law], Zeitschrift für Urheber- und Medienrecht [ZUM] 2012, 108 (2012).

Frank Huber, Kai Vollhardt & Frederick Meyer, Helden der Werbung? – Eine Untersuchung der Relevanz von Werbefiguren für das Konsumverhalten [Heroes of Advertisement? – Research on the Relevance of Spokes-Characters for Consumers' Behaviour], Marketing volume 31, no. 03, (2009).

Annette Kur, Der wettbewerbliche Leistungsschutz – Gedanken zum wettbewerbsrechtlichen Schutz von Formgebungen, bekannten Marken und "Characters"[Protection under Competition Law – Thoughts on the Protection of Shapes, Famous Marks and Characters], GRUR 1990, 1.

Frank Lotze, Markenmaskottchen – Warum wir bestimmte Werbefiguren nie vergessen [Spokescharacters – Why Certain Marketing Characters are Never Forgotten], Welt am Sonntag, Jul 22nd 2012.

Ralf Mäder, Messung und Steuerung von Markenpersönlichkeit: Entwicklung eines Messinstruments und Anwendung in der Werbung mit prominenten Testimonials (Schriftenreihe des Instituts für Marktorientierte Unternehmensführung (IMU), Universität Mannheim), (2005).

Matthias Meyer, Character Merchandising, Der Schutz fiktiver Figuren als Marke [Character Merchandising, the Protection of Fictitious Characters as Trade Marks], Europäische Hochschulschriften: Reihe 2, Rechtswissenschaft, volume 3668.

OHIM – The Manual Concerning Opposition.

Proposal for a Directive of the European Parliament and of the Council to Approximate the Laws of the Member States Relating to Trade marks, COM (2013) 162 final, 2013/0089 (COD), (proposed 2013).

Heijo Ruijsenaars, Overview of the Legal Aspects of Merchandising in Character Merchandising in Europe (Heijo Ruijsenaars ed., 2003).

Heijo Ruijsenaars, Workshop No. 6 – Character Merchandising, AIPPI Y.B. 1992/III, 348.

Christian Scherz & Susanne Bergmann, Character Merchandising in Germany in Character Merchandising in Europe (Heijo Ruijsenaars ed., 2003), 127-143.

Ilanah Simon, How does "Essential Function" Drive European Trade Mark Law? What is the Essential Function of a Trade Mark? 2005 IIC 401.

Clemens Thiele, Urheberrechtlicher Schutz für Kunstfiguren – von Odysseus bis Lara Croft, (IRIS – Rechtliche Rundschau der europäischen, audiovisellen Informationsstelle), (2004).

3. International

Heijo Ruijsenaars, *The WIPO Report on Character Merchandising*, Int'l. Rev. of Intell. Prop. and Competition Law [IIC] 1994, 532 (1994).

World Intellectual Property Organisation (WIPO), Character Merchandising – Report prepared by the International Bureau, WO/INF/108 (1994).

IV. Treatises

1. United States of America

Louis Altman & Mara Pollack, Callman on Unfair Competition, Trademarks and Monopolies (Thomson Reuthers 2013);

Jerome Gilson, Anne Gilson Laldone & Karin Green, Gilson on Trademarks (83d ed., 2013).

David Hilliard, Joseph Welch & Uli Widmaier, Trademarks and Unfair Competition (8 ed. 2010).

William Landes & Rrichard Posner, The Economic Structure of Intellectual Property Law (Harvard University Press 2003).

J. Thomas McCarthy, McCarthy on Trademarks and Unfair Competition (4th ed., 1996-2013).

Horwitz, Ethan, World Trademark Law and Practice (2d ed., 1985-2013).

2. European Union

Adams, John N., Character Merchandising (1996).

3. Germany

Karl-Heinz Fezer, Markenrecht (4th ed. 2009).

Thomas Dreier & Gernot Schulze, Urheberrechtsgesetz: UrhG, (4th ed., 2013).

Friedrich Fromm & Wilhelm Nordemann, Urheberrecht (10 ed. 2008).

Wolfgang Gloy, Michael Losschelder & Willi Edelmann, Handbuch des Wettbewerbsrechts (4 ed. 2010).

4. International

Georg Bodenhausen, Guide to the Application of the Paris Convention for the Protection of Industrial Property (BIRPI 1969).

Paul Goldstein & P. Berndt Hugenholtz, International Copyright: Principles, Law and Practice (2d ed. 2010).